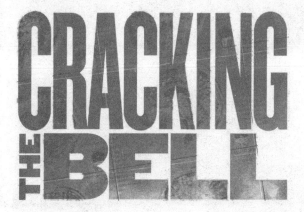

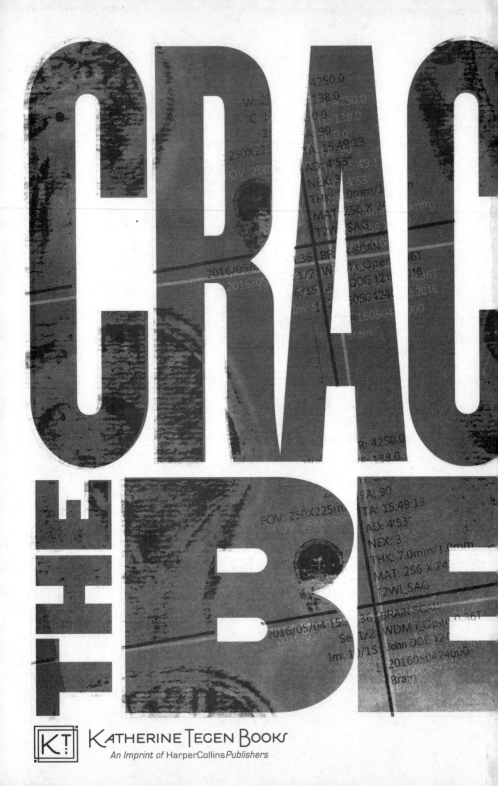

THE CRAC

BE

KATHERINE TEGEN BOOKS

An Imprint of HarperCollins Publishers

Katherine Tegen Books is an imprint of HarperCollins Publishers.

Cracking the Bell
www.epicreads.com
Library of Congress Control Number: 2019938848
ISBN 978-0-06-245314-3
Typography by Joel Tippie
19 20 21 22 23 PC/LSCH 10 9 8 7 6 5 4 3 2 1
❖
First Edition

To Marty, Chris, Jeremy, Frank, JD, Pete, Rod, Dirk, Ben, Mike, and everyone I played the game with.

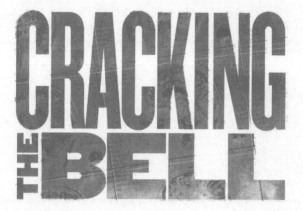

CHAPTER 1

SEPTEMBER 28: CRACKING THE BELL

Football has been my medicine. It has given me a singularity of purpose. It is the tower I built, on which I stand and see everything around me.

I'm a defensive player, but that doesn't mean football is simple seek and destroy, like some people might think. I captain the defense, which takes smarts, especially the way I play the game. I'm not some firing missile. I'm a smart bomb, communicating subtly, like through fungal mycelium, to a network of other smart bombs, my killer teammates.

On the field the world goes into vignette mode on Instagram. I'm in this dark tunnel except for a brightly lit place right in the center where everything makes sense. I shout an alignment, read how the offense sets up, call out adjustments—verbally, with my eyes, with hand gestures—signal plays to watch for, react to action in the backfield, take on blocks.

The world makes sense on the football field.

Even on September 28, apparently. In fact, as soon as we left the locker room, my bone-tired heaviness, my thoughts of my sister, Hannah, and poor Mom and Grandpa John . . . they went away and all there was in front of me was grass, jersey, helmet, the mechanics of Lancaster's offense lit in a bright Instagram vignette.

Screw Lancaster. I'm not a kind person on the football field. Yes, I play smart. But after I make my reads, I am free to destroy.

In the fourth quarter of a heavyweight bout that featured far more defense than offense, we led Lancaster by six points.

But as time fled, Lancaster had the ball.

They are really good. They are the monsters of the Southwest Wisconsin Conference. They drove the length of the field—their huge linemen, having finally exhausted our front seven, paved the way for Jimi Jentz and Jake Brogley, their fleet-footed running backs. With just over a minute left, they moved all the way down to our twenty-two yard line. But I didn't lose faith. I knew this business. I knew my place in it.

I'd studied so much film. I had a research paper full of evidence proving they got conservative when they hit this part of the field. Most teams who played them lost confidence, lost their will to fight. Most teams got run over easily. Why would Lancaster do anything risky? Most teams laid down and lost.

Not us.

In the huddle, I was my most pure "second life" self. I nodded, looked into everybody's eyes, pointed at each one of my teammates. "Not us. Not us. They will not run us over," I said. "We bend. We don't break."

My teammates huffed and snorted. They nodded, returned my gaze.

"Let's go. Now," I said.

And I was right about conservative. Of course. Lancaster called running alignments three plays in a row, certain we'd lay down. But each time, I lined us up like a hammer poised to hit. They couldn't move at all. One yard first play. A yard loss second. No gain third.

My heart pounded. The vignette was blinding.

Dave Dieter, our defensive coordinator, pumped his fist, gave me the thumbs-up. Very few knew, but Dieter let me call most of the game by myself. Essentially, Dieter was cheerleading, and I did his coordinator job.

On fourth down, Lancaster had to go for it, even though they had ten yards to go. There was no other choice. Images from the film I'd watched riffled through my mind. I knew that their playbook would open up in this situation. A pass was coming, and I knew which one.

Then Coach Dieter tried to grab the defensive reins. He signaled in a set, shouted for the corners to stay back off the line of scrimmage.

I shook my head, tried to shake him off.

Dieter signaled the set again.

"Ignore Dieter," I said in the huddle. "Don't play off the line. It's an option route to Clay. He's the guy, right?"

Everyone nodded.

"Press on the damn edges."

"You sure, man?" Matty Weber, the free safety, asked.

"Can't have Clay running to the damn sideline. We don't want him stopping the clock if he gets a first down. Make him cross in front of me," I said. "Funnel him right at me."

The corners nodded. They broke huddle. They lined up tight.

"Back off! Back off!" Coach Dieter screamed.

My heart slowed. I crouched.

"Back off!" Coach Dieter cried. Our corners didn't budge.

"Red. Red. Red," Lancaster's quarterback shouted. "Hut. Hut!"

Dakota Clay, Lancaster's all-state tight end, got bumped off the line by our outside linebacker, Knutson. It was happening just like I thought it would. Our corner was between the hash and the sideline and Matty Weber was shaded to that side to double Clay. Instead of running out and up the field, Clay rode the bump and dragged across the middle.

I stayed crouched, made myself small, baited Lancaster's QB into thinking the middle of the field was open. It worked perfectly. Lancaster had spent the entire game running every play away from me, keeping me from being a factor. Not this time. The QB threw the ball. It left his hand on target, right at Clay. I exploded forward, accelerated like rockets were attached to my ass. I didn't break down for the tackle at all, because I knew exactly where the ball would be. At the last moment, I uncoiled on Dakota Clay. I exploded into him at the same moment the ball reached his hands. It was brutal, crushing, like a pickup truck blowing a country intersection. Clay cried out. The ball bounced away. The crowd leaped to its feet, screaming.

Even though a few seconds remained on the clock, all we had to do to win was take a knee. Game over.

After the hit, apparently Clay lay on the field groaning.

I didn't hear that part. I'd done something I shouldn't do. Really bad technique, failed to keep my eyes up, dropped my head down when I made the hit.

Eyes down. Head down. Absolutely terrible technique.

I have a tendency to drop my head when I want a hit to be remembered. Once in my career, sophomore year, the resultant collision caused my eyes to roll back in my head, my sinuses to drain, and my ears to ring like a French cathedral on Sunday morning. No, not just bells. I heard the shriek of a witch for the first time. I'd worked hard to counter my intuitive style of play after sophomore year and had avoided that kind of collision, although I did hear the shriek of a witch one other time, junior year, when a receiver cracked back on me, hit me at full speed while I wasn't looking. Man, I worked so hard to avoid that kind of contact.

I'll tell you this, I'd never dropped my eyes on a 240-pound superathlete before. The back of my helmet had ricocheted off Clay's ribs and shot my face down into the turf. Crash. For a count of three, I think, I was totally out (looked like that on the video—Kirby Sheldon showed me later). Twiggs ran onto the field and raised his arms, signaled the coaches for help, because for that three count I looked dead. But before anyone could check on me, I was awake. I pushed myself off the turf and ran to the sideline like nothing had happened. On film my teammates slapped me on the helmet, jumped up and down, and high-fived each other around me.

I don't remember it.

This is what I remember: witch whistles screamed in my ears. What sound would steel make if it was torn apart slowly? Witch whistles. Got more intense. The whistles came from ten places at first, then combined and became a single dying girl shrieking without breathing. Constant deadly shriek. The sky above turned orange, yellow, blue, red . . .

What's happening? What's happening?

That's the last thing I remember thinking. Or seeing. Or hearing. The last thing for many hours. I don't remember the good-game line, or hugging Dad and Grandma Gin in the stands, or riding the bus back to the high school, or telling Twiggs and Riley I had to go home to see Mom, because she hadn't made it to the game, or driving home, or going to bed, or getting up and vomiting.

All that was gone from my head, my cracked bell leaking it away. The contents of my second life leaking away.

CHAPTER 2

FOUR YEARS AGO, IN JULY: HANNAH DIED

Because Grace, who was my girlfriend back when I was an eighth-grade criminal, works for Grandma Gin at Dairy Queen, Mom wouldn't let me work there anymore. To make money, I clean gutters and paint houses with Joey Derossi, a twenty-year-old dude who was my sister Hannah's weirdest friend.

He is a wild card but isn't wild. He's just weird and I like him more than just about anybody, not only because he reminds me of how funny Hannah was.

In my second life, we drove around in his old GMC pickup truck. He played whatever music he'd gotten into (usually from the 1960s or '70s, but sometimes new stuff—as long as he could get it on CD or cassette—Joey lives as analogue as possible, no smartphone, electronic notebook, laptop, internet). He talked about whatever strange idea he'd been reading about at the library. Last summer, he began asking me to write stuff and read it to him. He wanted to examine my deep perceptions. Doing that writing—and I wrote all the time—felt good, but also shook me up. Yes, I like Joey Derossi more than anyone my age, except for maybe Grace.

This is how the weird writing thing started.

Last summer, after I began having a recurring Hannah dream, Joey gave me one of those green-and-white composition notebooks you can get at Walmart for a dollar. He said, "Grab a pen. Write that shit out. Write about your feelings, bro. This is the greatest gift the great eyeball in the sky gave to all us humanoid primates down here. The ability to reflect and write out all our big-brained-ape shit."

"Seriously?" I said. "I don't really want to."

"I'm your pal, man. Listen to your pal," he said.

"No thanks," I said, handing the green notebook back to him.

"Bullshit. Riggles and Twine don't care if you're struggling. But your real pal, aka me, wants you to be as mentally healthy as you are physically magnificent."

Joey Derossi. A freak of nature. I did think it was funny he called my best friends over at school, Riley and Twiggs, "Riggles and Twine." I also thought maybe he was right about this gift from the "great eyeball in the sky" (this is what he called his version of God). When my first life broke completely, back when I was fourteen, the social worker at the group home I was sent to asked me to write stuff, too.

Anyway, this is the first thing I wrote for Joey Derossi. I started writing it in first person, because why wouldn't I write about myself in first person? But Joey—who is probably a genius—made me go back and write it in third person.

"That way you get out of your own path. You gotta get out of your damn head!"

Okay . . .

Four years ago in July, Hannah Died

The phone rang just after 10 p.m. Isaiah's mom and dad were in the living room watching a Kevin Costner movie on Netflix. Something about baseball, which thirteen-year-old Isaiah thought was stupid. This was during the summer between seventh and eighth grade, when Isaiah was small and dirty and liked to eat peanut butter right out of the jar (sometimes with his finger).

Instead of watching the stupid movie with his boring parents, he played Temple Run II *on his phone. Although he was physically attracted to Scarlett Fox—the character with whom he played the game—he kind of hated* Temple Run II. *It took too long to die once you got good and when you did die you had to start over from the beginning, so it took a long time to learn how to deal with the challenge that killed you. It gave him a big headache. Sadly,* Temple Run II *was one of the few games that still worked on his*

*piece-of-shit Galaxy, and he needed to be doing something
with his damn brain.*

*There was tension in the air. His sister, Hannah, who
had always been the good kid in the family, had skipped
her shift at Dairy Queen to go to Blackhawk Lake with her
new boyfriend, Ray Gatos. The dude seemed so nerdy to
Isaiah. But apparently Ray had some criminal intentions?
Or a criminal mind? That's what Isaiah's parents said anyway.*

*"That kid is a bad influence," Mom whispered before
the movie started. "We better keep our eye on him."*

*It really didn't seem possible to his parents that Han-
nah would have chosen criminal behavior, missing her
DQ shift, on her own. Grandma Gin owned Dairy Queen.
Hannah hadn't just skipped out on a fast-food job; she'd
put her own grandma into a crap spot on a busy summer
night (Isaiah had been forced to work for two hours, which
made him mad, except the new girl, Grace, was at Dairy
Queen, and he liked her weird sense of humor and also, if
forced to admit it, how she smelled when she was sweaty),
and Grandma Gin was not one to forgive and forget, so
Hannah would be in trouble for a long time. . . .*

*Hannah wouldn't invite the wrath of Grandma Gin into
her life, would she?*

*Scarlett Fox, who looked a little like the new girl,
Grace—kind of pouty and pointy—burst through the temple ruins, jumping over massive holes, sliding under fallen*

trees and bursts of fire, picking up all the tiles, and avoiding the giant creature that chased her and wanted to tear her to pieces.

The landline rang in the kitchen. Isaiah figured it was Hannah, finally. He didn't even look up from his phone. He didn't want to hear Mom's screaming. But Isaiah did look up when Mom failed to scream. At first, Mom said yes, yes, yes? Then she gasped. Then she began to cry oh no, oh no, oh no, again and again.

"What?" Isaiah asked. "What?" he shouted from his bedroom.

"You know there's no way Ray Gatos forced Hannah to go, right?" Joey said to me after I read it aloud to him. "No way he was the one pushing her. It was other way around with those guys. Ray Gatos was like a cute little teddy bear Hannah carried around with her. Bro, she owned Ray Gatos."

"Really?" I asked.

"Yeah, man. Yeah. All you people think Hannah was some angel, but she wasn't, okay? Don't get me wrong, she was about as nice as a human being could be. She was sweet to a weird-ass high schooler like I was, right? But come on. She was fun. Hannah was, like, 'Hannah the Adventurer.' She was a little bit half-cocked and good to go, you know what I'm saying?"

"No."

"She loved to live her life. That's all. Nothing evil. She was just out there doing stuff."

"That's a new perspective," I said.

"Always good to see things from different angles, bro. How about you imagine her at the end, in that car, loving life, not worried about breaking those rules too much?"

So I did. One Saturday afternoon two weeks before football started, while we were out in Hazel Green working for an old lady Joey had known since he was a kid, Joey cleaned gutters on a ladder above. I sat on the old lady's lawn with my green notebook and wrote this . . .

Ray Gatos drives his Toyota Corolla on the rolling county road. "I can't believe your grandma let you off work tonight," he says.

"Yeah. Ha ha. Seriously," Hannah, who sits next to him, replies. She blushes. She is not a great liar. She doesn't want Ray to worry she might get in trouble. To take her mind off things, she sticks her hand out the window and lets it ride the hot air currents of a falling summer night. Whatever trouble she'll be in, the day was worth it. The whole day had been amazing. Grandma couldn't hate her forever, right?

At that same moment, Steven Hartley (33), leaves the Boulder Junction Tap and stumbles to his new Ford F-150. The man is broken, drunk, loaded to the hilt. He climbs in, turns the ignition, and puts his head down on the steering wheel. "I can't do it," he sobs. Then he takes a big breath, lifts his big head, whispers, "Screw this." He flips the truck into drive.

Meanwhile, the sun sets red over the Driftless Area, that weird, rolling landscape in southwest Wisconsin that the earth-grading glaciers somehow missed. Everything runs red to orange and green in the fields and a perfect light shivers along the road.

Ray and Hannah have not been drinking, like some of their friends were out by the lake. They're not about that. They are quiet, and totally in love. They swam together in the lake. They hiked down into a valley and up across a high ridge that gave them a view of the entire park. They kissed up there for the first time.

And now, in the car, they listen to Sufjan Stevens, the Michigan *album, because it's Hannah's favorite, because the sweet, rolling songs remind Hannah of home, of rolling Wisconsin country. The open windows let hot farm air pour in, wet earth, growing corn. It is perfect. Her hand rides the currents.*

Ray's Corolla crests a hill near Rewey, about fifteen miles northeast of Bluffton. The song "Alanson, Crooked River" comes on. It's not even a real song, just a dozen tiny bells ringing together, like the sound fairies would make playing in the tall grasses along the road. "I love this," Hannah says.

They cross into an intersection. The pickup truck driven by Steven Hartley comes from the right, runs a stop sign. Hannah doesn't even have time to scream. In a flash of steel and light, Steven Hartley's truck blows the Corolla to hell.

Steven Hartley of Arthur, Wisconsin, dies in a blink. He's so confused as the Ford's engine cuts through him.

He has a blood alcohol level of .19, which is more than twice the legal limit. He is in the middle of a divorce. He has a two-year-old daughter named Melanie. Everyone is confused. The dude never drank. Never.

Until he went to Boulder Junction Tap. Then he did drink.

He kills Hannah while fairy bells play.

I read my thing to Joey while he drove us home from Hazel Green.

He had to pull over.

He stared out the window for five minutes without saying a word.

Finally, he looked at me, and said, "Yeah, bro. I bet that's exactly how it happened. You nailed it. The goddamn fairy bells, right?"

CHAPTER 3

SEPTEMBER 29: MORNING AFTER THE FOOTBALL GAME

I awoke thinking about my written version of Hannah's crash. Or trying to. I kept sort of passing out. I wanted to remember it. I rolled to get out of bed. I couldn't. I reached for my green notebook, which was stuck under my bed. But the room spun and the woman, the witch, stirred, shrieked. I couldn't get my fingers around my notebook's edges. I rolled back onto my pillow, swallowed hard. I had a terrible taste in my mouth. My head pounded.

What is going on? What is going on?

I shut my eyes tight. *I am injured.*

Shrieking, like the sound of a girl losing her life?

Hannah is dead.

The bell had cracked.

15

CHAPTER 4

SEPTEMBER 29: INTO THE KITCHEN

I stumbled into the kitchen, looking for coffee, hoping caffeine would help steady me, quiet the noise of my broken bell. I touched the walls in the hall; I touched the doorframe of the bathroom. I could feel things, but nothing felt real, substantial, like my soul had been knocked out of the universe and what was left was all plastic.

Mom sat at the table in the corner. She looked up from her iPad. She seemed normal.

September 28—the worst day of the year in my family—had passed. The day before she had canceled all her client meetings. She's a small-town lawyer and needs to be able to think straight. The day before she had stood in the yard staring out into space. The day before, September 28, would've been

Hannah's twenty-first birthday. The day before, September 28, was the fifth anniversary of my grandpa John's death.

Mom couldn't function on September 28.

Generally, I couldn't either. Usually, I took the day off school, so I, too, could stare into space, except I couldn't the day before, because I'd had a football game to play.

Mom squinted her eyes at me. It was September 29, and she was back inside herself, reading newspapers on her iPad, sitting at the little kitchen table.

This was a normal Saturday-morning scene, but things weren't normal. Generally, on Saturday mornings during football season, Mom, like so many Wisconsinites, a lifelong football fan, was chatty. We'd drink coffee together and run through the events of the previous evening's game.

But she squinted at me and said nothing.

"Hey," I said. My voice sounded fake. It echoed and whistled through gray corners.

Mom didn't say anything.

"What?" I asked. Echoes and whistles.

"I heard you last night," she replied.

"What did you hear? The witches?" I surprised myself by saying that. But I could hear the witches.

"Witches?"

"Not real witches."

"I heard you vomiting, Isaiah."

I paused. Tried to remember. "I don't think so."

"You don't remember? That is even more disgusting."

The witch noise grew. A shady image emerged. Falling on the thick carpet in my bedroom, crawling into the bathroom, pulling myself up and over the cold side of the bowl. "Oh yeah. I guess. Vomited," I said.

"Three times," Mom hissed.

"I was sick, I guess."

"You were wasted."

"Wasted? No," I said. The girl's cry got louder. "I don't drink."

"I asked you if you had been drinking and you said yes."

"Last night?"

"When else, goddamn it?"

"We talked?"

"More like I screamed, and you crawled away from me."

"No. I didn't drink. That didn't happen."

She shook her head. Her eyes watered. "Isaiah. I don't care if you win a goddamn football game. You cannot do that and live in this house. You will not behave like that in my . . ."

"I would *not* drink," I said. "What time did I get home?"

Mom cocked her head. "Early. Someone must've had a bottle in the locker room."

"No one would do that. Do you know my teammates, Mom?"

"I thought I did," she said.

"Something else happened. I . . . I didn't drink, Mom. I wouldn't."

"What do you mean? Something happened? During the game?"

I nodded. The witches screamed.

"Grandma Gin said you were down on the field for a bit?"

"I don't remember," I said. "I can't . . ."

Mom pushed back her chair. Anger left. Concern spread across her face. "What's wrong with you, Isaiah?"

"I would never drink, Mom," I said.

"Isaiah?"

Wind ripped through the corners. Witches cried. "I have to lie down."

Mom stood.

I slid to the floor, leaned against a cupboard door. "I really don't feel good."

CHAPTER

BEFORE FOOTBALL

Joey remembers me from the days of my criminal life pretty well. He said I seemed like a normal kid, but I wasn't. Joey hated Reid Schmidt and Ben Carpenter, my only friends back then. "Those dudes were shit. Reid shoved me into a corner over at Kwik Trip back when I was still in school. Bastard held me there and burped in my face. What a damn pig."

I wrote this for Joey in my green notebook. It's about my first life.

When Isaiah was a kid, he was the anti-Hannah. Hannah was a neat freak. She was sparky and funny. He was not funny. He was grubby and he broke stuff and he got in fistfights at the swimming pool and he didn't like school, so he did terribly, and so some of the same middle school teachers who had loved Tammy Bertram (his mom) when she was a perfect seventh grader laid into her about her terrible, gross kid. Mom sent him to his room when she got home from parent-teacher conferences because she couldn't bear to look at him. Hannah was so easy to brag about, so clearly her mother's child. But the dirty little caveman, Isaiah? What a pain in the ass.

That's what Mom called him before Hannah died, the caveman. It was sort of a pet name. Until it wasn't.

Isaiah did something at Hannah's visitation. It was a closed casket visitation because Hannah was crushed to pieces and badly burnt and so the "restorative" work that needed to be done to make her presentable was too much for the mortician in town.

But the casket was out there on some kind of podium, right at chest level for Isaiah. There were no flowers on it. Nothing. Just the door. Not good.

Before all the people—the high school kids, and teachers, and his mom's law clients and his dad's colleagues, the staff and professors from the college—showed up to stand in line, to come forward and grimly shake Grandma Gin's hand and Mom's hand and Dad's hand, to tell the family how much they would miss Hannah, Isaiah fixated on the casket, on the fact that his dead sister, who he loved so much because she was hilarious and her eyes sparkled with glee when she chased him around the house, was inside it, and he couldn't control himself. He could never control himself. He wanted to say sorry, to say goodbye to her. He

21

stood up from the folding chair and went to it and lifted the casket door and looked in.

He began to shake. He began to cry. What was that thing inside?

Why didn't they have the box locked shut? Why was the box even out there at the visitation? Why didn't anybody pay attention to the thirteen-year-old kid who constantly did stupid things? Who was skin and bone and vibrating energy all the damn time? Who would miss Hannah more than everyone else combined? Who had impulse control problems in the first place?

He screamed.

Grandma Gin grabbed for Isaiah. The casket door slammed. He fought Grandma off. Dad grabbed for him. Isaiah fought him, too. He couldn't say why he fought. He couldn't say anything. He was blind with fear and rage.

And then Mom lost her mind. She started screaming, shrieking. "Get him out of here! Get that piece of shit out of here!"

Isaiah ran. He found his way to Pine Street and then down to the grocery store, a half mile away. He hid behind piles of flattened cardboard boxes by a dumpster filled with rotting vegetables. He crouched down, dropped his head between his knees. He sobbed and sobbed and sobbed.

A grocery store worker found him when it was dark. The cops came to pick him up. No one spoke to him at home. He didn't go to the funeral the next day.

A year later, Isaiah had grown physically, and things

were off the rails. The cops picked him up many times. He smoked pot at school in the eighth-grade hall bathrooms. He got wasted repeatedly with two young dickheads, Reid Schmidt and Ben Carpenter. He was arrested for shop-lifting at Walmart (box of Combos pretzel snacks—not that big a deal, one would think). Later, after he drank a half bottle of vodka by himself and vandalized his own house, he was sent to live in a group home in Muscoda, Wisconsin, for two months (where he learned to smoke menthol cigarettes and to fight with kids much bigger and older and then also to breathe through his nose, to calm himself, to talk in group therapy, to write about his feelings). But when he got back from Muscoda, after prom-ising to never drink again (he'd meant it), he followed that messed-up Grace again—because he couldn't help it—to a massive party in a cornfield, which got busted, and he got hauled to jail again, and he received the ultimatum.

"Go out for football or go to Muscoda for good," Dad said.

What would his life have been like if he had gone to Muscoda?

Where would he be?

"Maybe he'd be happier?" Joey asked.

"No. I love football," I said.

"Life is more than football, bro," Joey said.

"No," Isaiah said. "Not really. It really isn't."

23

CHAPTER

SEPTEMBER 29: THE HOSPITAL

"Witch whistles? Is this the first time you've heard these witch whistles in your head?" the emergency room doctor asked me.

I didn't want to answer honestly. A little voice inside me said, *Shut up. Do you know what you're doing to yourself?* but the actual voice in my throat said, "No. Not the first time."

Mom, who still wore her cheesed-out Mickey Mouse T-shirt and sweatpants that she used as pajamas, tipped her head to the side. "Are you saying you've hit your head like that more than once, Isaiah?"

"No . . . no. Not like that," I mumbled. "Not like last night."

Mom had a leather-covered notebook with her, taking notes. She scribbled in it like crazy.

"What are you writing?" I asked.

Dad, who left us two years ago, but had driven over from his crappy little apartment, looked at his phone, read headlines in the *New York Times*, which is probably what he would've been doing at his own place, said, "She's taking notes so she can use this conversation against you some time in the future. The regime keeps meticulous records."

"Oh, come on. Not now, Dan," Mom said.

"How often have you heard the witch whistling?" the doctor asked.

"Not very often."

"Give me a number. How many times?"

"Two, three times if you count last night. I've heard ringing in my ears other times, maybe six times, total," I said.

Dad looked up from his phone. "Are you serious, Isaiah?" Dad said. "That's not good."

No one spoke for a moment. Mom didn't take notes.

We'd already established that the concussion was more than minor—my pupils were normal, but I admitted that I might have been knocked out and that I couldn't remember coming home. We'd established that I'd have to take a minimum of a week off without doing anything sports-related to rest and recover, and that I'd need to visit the clinic on the following Friday to be reassessed.

All that was okay with me, I thought. It helped that the next week represented a soft spot in our schedule. River Valley, our next opponent, hadn't won a game all season. Twiggs, Riley, and the rest would be okay without me.

That was good. All my body wanted was to lie in a dark, quiet room.

But the energy changed when I mentioned witch whistles.

"Have you ever lost consciousness before last night?" the doctor asked.

"No?" I said, but it sounded like a question, not a definitive answer.

"How do you usually feel?" the doctor asked. "When you hear the ringing?"

"Just the ringing? Good. I feel good, usually."

"Good?" Mom asked.

"Well, that sounds good, doesn't it?" Dad asked.

"Not necessarily," the doctor said.

"Explain 'good,'" Mom said.

"Better. My sinuses drain, and I can breathe really well and I'm awake and I feel faster, feel ready to go again."

"Sounds like a meth addiction," Dad said.

"Stop, Dan," Mom said.

The doctor squinted at me. "You are the one doing the hitting, but you're the one getting injured?"

I wanted to leave, to sleep.

"That's what's happening," Mom said. She scribbled a note.

"Can you avoid that kind of contact when you play?" the doctor asked.

"I just need to keep my eyes up. I'm getting better at that technique."

"Huh?" the doctor said. "You're mumbling, Isaiah."

"Eyes what?" Mom asked.

"Up. Up," I said.

"What, Isaiah?" Dad asked.

The doctor shook his head. "If Isaiah were my child, I wouldn't let him play anymore."

"What?" I asked.

"Because of the long-term neurological impacts?" Dad asked.

"Not just that," the doctor said.

"I want to go home," I said.

"Please explain," Mom said.

Before speaking, the doctor sighed. "Well, it's rare," he said.

"What is?" Dad asked.

"But suffering two major concussions within a short period of time can result in *second impact syndrome*. . . ."

Mom scribbled furiously.

"That's just obvious," I mumbled. "And three major concussion within a short period of time can result in *third impact syndrome. Fourth fourth. Fifth fifth.*"

The doctor talked over me. ". . . and just look at him, and with Isaiah's propensity to take contact . . ."

"*Sixth sixth,*" I said.

"Be quiet, Isaiah," Mom said. "What is *second impact syndrome?*"

"We're not sure, *exactly*," the doctor said.

"*Seventh seventh,*" I said.

"Be quiet. What is wrong with you?" Mom said.

"But catastrophic head injuries in football are associated with a recent, prior head trauma in nearly three-quarters of the cases. He is in bad shape now, but the second impact is the dangerous one."

Mom scribbled.

"What results from a catastrophic head injury?" Dad asked. "Impaired thinking?"

"*Eighth eighth,*" I said.

"Goddamn it," Mom said. "Stop."

Everyone looked at me, concerned. I should maybe have been concerned, too, as this "out-of-turn talking" was out of character.

The moment passed.

"Catastrophic head injury results in death." The doctor looked at me. "Or worse."

There was a moment of total silence.

"What's worse than death?" I asked.

"What, Isaiah?" Dad asked. "Why are you mumbling?"

"What is worse than death?" I shouted, the volume rattling around in my broken head.

"A vegetative state, I think," the doctor said. "A coma."

"Oh God," Mom said.

"That's why I'd be very careful if he were my child," the doctor said.

CHAPTER 7

SEPTEMBER 30: MORNING

The next morning, I lay in bed and listened to silence in my head. So quiet. I'd slept for seventeen hours straight. It was a relief to hear silence. No girl crying, no witch whistles, no bell ringing, no nothing. But I didn't feel right, still. I felt numb and exhausted.

In my second life, my football life, Sundays are days I give to other people. It starts with Grandma Gin. I drive her to the ten o'clock church service. Then, if there's a noon Packers game, we stay at her house. Mom comes over. We eat brats or lasagna or something. I help Grandma do chores in the yard or in the house. Later in the day, I go to Dad's apartment. Twiggs often joins me there for food and Sunday-night football, and we do some homework, too.

I loved my Sundays. I loved my time with Grandma, even the church part, because the pastor is smart and funny. I enjoyed listening to him.

But on that Sunday, the idea of getting up, getting out of bed, showering, putting on clothes tighter fitting than gym shorts? Felt impossible. I could barely move.

So, I was pleased when Mom knocked on my door and said, "I called Grandma. I told her you were sick, couldn't make it today."

"Good, thanks. Maybe we can still go over and watch the Packers with her later."

"Sure, Isaiah. I probably won't. I've got some work. But you can if you're feeling like it."

The light from the hallway haloing Mom bothered me, so I turned over and faced the wall.

"Isaiah?" Mom asked.

"Yeah?"

"I would like it if you got up, though. Maybe we can go to Country Kitchen for breakfast?"

"I don't know. I don't think I want to." We did lots of breakfasts at Country Kitchen, and I loved them, but the idea made me sick now.

"No. It's important to me," Mom said. "I'd like us to talk this morning."

I breathed deep. I did not want to go.

"Start moving," Mom said. "You'll feel better."

Even though I felt like an empty candy wrapper left in an old winter coat pocket, I knew the real me, should that Isaiah ever return to my body, would want to convince Mom that everything was all right so she wouldn't worry. "I do feel better," I said. "Just sleepy."

Twenty minutes later, we drove across town to Country Kitchen. I tried to be normal.

"Was Grandma Gin mad that I wasn't picking her up for church?"

"No. She said she might skip herself. Apparently last week's sermon irritated her."

"I know," I said. "I was there."

"What liberal assault did the pastor unleash?" Mom asked.

"Something from the New Testament. Like, blessed are the peacemakers or something."

"Ha. What a communist."

"Threat to American values, he is," I said.

Easily a third of my conversations with Mom involved making jokes about Grandma Gin's "political conservatism." My aunt Melinda left her husband a couple years ago because she got romantically involved with a woman (she's still with her—Judy Gunderson—she's a nurse in the hospital in La Crosse where Melinda works). Grandma Gin took Melinda's husband's side. Grandma Gin won't speak to Melinda, which has caused another break in a family full of brokenness. Still, it felt like a lie to make easy political jokes about Grandma like that, but the jokes filled Mom with glee, so I participated. If Grandpa John were still around, things would be different.

In the restaurant, we sat in one of those little two-person booths. Squeezed in. I tried to choke down the bacon, broccoli, and cheese omelet I'd ordered, even though it tasted like sand. I felt like strewn garbage shivering in the wind. It didn't help that Mom was silent the moment we sat down. Her eyes stayed glued to a spot a few inches left of my forehead. She was very still while I shook. She didn't eat her sausage-and-onion scramble. Finally, after I finished choking down my breakfast, I felt obligated to engage.

I tried to focus the thoughts in my cracked bell, picked up a piece of raisin toast, and pointed it at her. I used the jokey tone that she appreciates. "Sooo . . . you wanted to talk? Better do that before I pass out from this butter overdose."

She sniffed. "That's right," she said. "You're right. I'm just having a hard time with this."

"With what?"

"Isaiah, you know how much I've been through in the last five years."

"I do. It's been bad."

"I've lost so much." She shook her head. "Too much for a woman my age."

"I know."

"And now you hear witch whistles in your head? Witch whistles, Isaiah? What the hell is that?"

"I don't hear the whistles very often."

"That's not what you told the doctor yesterday."

"Really. I hear whistling very rarely." I didn't mention the

32

girl screaming or the pounding or the ringing or the winds that whipped dried grasses and garbage.

Mom turned. She looked out the window to her right. "You should never hear whistles in your head." She swallowed, took in a sharp breath. "We have bad luck in this family. I don't know why. It's terrible. I'm so sorry."

"Sorry about what?" I said.

"You can't invite more bad luck. You can't just open the door wide."

"I'm not opening a door," I said.

She turned back, faced me. "Second impact syndrome, Isaiah?"

"What?"

"Death. Or permanent brain damage. This is what you get from football?"

"Millions of people play football, Mom. I'm not going to die."

"Some of them die, Isaiah!" Mom said, volume dialed up.

An old couple at the neighboring table paused midbite, like synchronized swimmers suddenly stuck in the middle of a routine. They turned toward us.

"Isaiah," Mom whispered. "I'm not going to let you die on a football field."

"I'm not going to die on a football field."

"That's right, because I'm not going to let you play anymore."

The old couple leaned toward us, to get their ears closer.

And I couldn't process. It didn't make sense.

"Really, honey. You can't play football anymore," she said quietly. "We don't know what you're doing to your brain. People die. Even later in life. People die from this. That man from the Bears? What's his name from San Diego? Junior Seau? People die. And you're hearing that brain damage in your head, sweetie. It's whistling at you. People really die."

"I know they die," I said. "I know lots of people die." The whistling rose. Wind ripped across ridges, picked up dust and sand. The crying rose.

Mom pulled in a breath through her nose. She sat up straight. "I can talk to Coach Reynolds, if you want. I can tell him what happened and why we've come to this decision. You don't have to bear the burden, Isaiah. I know this isn't easy. But your life is more valuable than a high school football game."

Crying witches. "We could win state," I said.

"Your life is more valuable than winning state," she said. "Do you want me to call Coach Reynolds? We can have him over this afternoon, if you want."

"No. Just wait. Just please let me think, okay?" I said. It wasn't just winning state. It was so much more than winning any game. It was my whole past. It was my future.

"Okay, but we've made this decision already. Do you understand?"

I shut my eyes. The room spun, accelerated, until it whipped around me, a tornado.

"We have to go home," I said.

CHAPTER

WHEN FOOTBALL STARTED

The whole weekend before the football season started, Joey Derossi kept telling me that my sport wasn't a big deal and I should stop making it such a big deal. So I wrote this:

> *"If you don't play, you go back to Muscoda. Your mother and I can't parent you."*
>
> *Isaiah and his dad sat in the front seat of Dad's car in the lot at the Belmont Tower County Park. Rain blasted down on the roof.*
>
> *"For how long?" Isaiah asked. He was scrawny, out of shape for a fourteen-year-old. He smoked menthol cigarettes, for God's sake.*
>
> *"Just give football a chance. I'm not saying you have to play forever."*

"No. How long would you send me up to Muscoda?"

Dad shook his head, shut his eyes. "You'll stay there until you go to prison or turn eighteen," he said.

Isaiah was a time bomb. You become what you do. He so often sought destruction he had become a bomb. "Fine," Isaiah said. "Muscoda it is."

"Wrong answer," Dad whispered. He let his forehead fall against the steering wheel.

The next morning, Dad drove Isaiah to the high school instead of to Muscoda. "Get out of the car," Dad said in the parking lot.

"And do what?" Isaiah asked.

"Go to the locker room and tell the coach you're here. Now. Get out."

Isaiah still isn't sure how it happened. Why didn't he just run off? Was there divine guidance? Who knows? But he did it. He got out, slammed the door, and walked one foot after the other into the coaches' offices.

He was terrified. He'd see classmates.

He hated Riley Johndrow—the muscle-headed blond kid—and Josh Penney—the curly-haired kid everyone called Twiggs due to his long arms and legs. Those guys were not only stupid; they had been mean to him, even in the terrible months after Hannah's death. In fact, one time the previous October, after Isaiah (who was a dick—he couldn't help it) tripped him in the hall, Riley Johndrow had grabbed Isaiah by the back of his shirt, flipped him

36

onto the ground, and put his forearm across his neck. He'd whispered to Isaiah, "I don't care if your sister did die. You mess with me again, and I will destroy you."

"You're pathetic, dude," Twiggs had said, standing above.

Even though it was the middle of the day, Isaiah had left the school building, wandered downtown.

Riley and Twiggs were as shocked to see Isaiah show up on the first day of freshman football practice as Isaiah was to be there. All the players in his class were shocked. Bluffton is a small enough town that they all knew what Isaiah was—a burner, a druggie, a rando.

Isaiah was treated as such by the equipment manager, who gave him a helmet that didn't fit right and shoulder pads that were too big. The Velcro on his belt was worn out, so his pants sagged. He looked like a little kid dressed up for Halloween.

A half hour later, the freshman coach, Mr. Trouten, used a language Isaiah didn't understand to describe what they'd be doing on that field.

Isaiah stared at the ground. Two days earlier he had been drunk in a cornfield, making out with Grace. And suddenly this? Dressed like an idiot in the August heat while a bunch of shit-smelling jocks stood around glaring at him?

Just walk away, Isaiah thought.

"Line up here, son," Coach Trouten said. He pointed to

the back of a line of kids.

Isaiah couldn't tell you why he went where Trouten had pointed. But one foot after another and there he was standing, waiting. There were giant pads (tackling dummies, he found out they were called) being held by assistant coaches (these young, muscular dudes from Bluffton College). Fear made Isaiah pay attention. The freshmen ballers in front of him did the following: On "go" (a coach shouted, go), they sprinted to the right, punched one of the big pads with both hands, then sprinted back to the left and decked the other dummy, tackled the thing, pushed themselves off the ground fast, and ran to the back of the line.

Isaiah now understands the drill simulates shedding a blocker (first dummy), then exploding into a ball carrier (second dummy). He had no idea what was going on then, though.

It came to his turn. His heart pounded. Adrenaline rose. He sprinted to the first dummy and didn't break down, just fell into it, then pushed himself off from on top of the dummy and sprinted to the other, leaped from too far away and hit the college assistant at the same time as the pad. The dude shouted, "Ow!" because Isaiah's helmet had crunched the guy's knuckles. Everyone laughed. Isaiah filled with rage (but also, oddly, felt some relief at hearing the coach's knuckles knock against the hard shell of the helmet).

While he waited in line for his next turn, Coach Trouten

came over and said, "Watch how Riley breaks down before he sheds the block." Isaiah watched Riley sprint up to the dummy, quickly crouch, then deliver the punches, before cutting hard and running through the other tackling dummy. "See how he uncoiled only when he got to the target? No jumping, son. Explosion on the ball carrier."

"Ball carrier," Isaiah said.

The next time through, Isaiah breathed deep through his nose to focus—something he had learned to do at the group home a month earlier. He heard go. He copied exactly what Riley had done. Sprint, crouch, punch, cut, sprint, uncoil. No one laughed this time. There was a distinct popping sound when Isaiah shed the blocker, another crisp pop when he hit the tackling dummy. In fact, there was actual quiet after his turn.

He didn't even have cleats yet. He wore Vans.

An hour later, when they did a live tackling drill, Isaiah uncoiled on a sophomore kid so hard the kid took a half minute to regain his breath. The silence was palpable. Coach Reynolds, who was the new varsity coach at the time, had been watching. "What's your name?" he asked (even though Isaiah's name was written on a piece of tape on his helmet).

"Isaiah Sadler," Isaiah mumbled.

"The evil one," Matty Weber whispered.

Coach Reynolds glared at Matty. Silence again. He turned back to Isaiah. "I talked to your father yesterday, right? I *understand why he wants you to play. Natural hitter."*

"Uh-huh," Isaiah said. And he felt pride, this glow, rise in his chest. He liked that feeling.

By the end of the first practice, everyone on the team was afraid of him and not because he was "the evil one." Riley came up to him in the locker room and said, "You're like Chuck Cecil." It was an obscure reference. No way Riley expected Isaiah to know that he was talking about a human missile, a safety (like Isaiah ended up being), who played for the Green Bay Packers in the late 1980s and early 1990s. But Grandma Gin's TV room was a Green Bay Packers shrine, and Isaiah had studied the football cards she kept in frames there. He'd read all the Packers yearbooks she'd collected.

"They called Cecil the Scud," Isaiah replied.

Riley stared at Isaiah for a moment, then said, "He was like a missile who sometimes missed. But when he hit, it was total destruction."

Isaiah nodded. "A Scud was a Russian missile. I googled that back in sixth grade because of Chuck Cecil. The Packers are very educational."

Riley smiled with the side of his mouth, nodded.

Isaiah suddenly didn't hate him. That was all it took.

A week later, Riley's dad began picking Isaiah up at 6 a.m. so he could lift weights with Riley and Twiggs, who made goofy-ass jokes, who Isaiah continued to hate until their third game, when Twiggs caught a touchdown pass with twenty-two seconds left, which beat Richland Center's freshman team by two. Then Isaiah loved him. The whole team piled on top of Twiggs in the back of the end zone, screaming for joy. They were flagged for unsportsmanlike conduct, but nobody cared. They couldn't help themselves.

After the fourth game, Isaiah asked Dad for a new phone number, so that his criminal friends, Ben and Reid, couldn't get ahold of him, so Grace couldn't text him. Dad took Isaiah to the Verizon store in Dubuque.

And Isaiah felt new. He began running gassers after weight lifting, began watching football on TV all weekend (college with Dad on Saturdays, pro with Grandma and Mom on Sundays), began playing Madden with Riley and Twiggs until midnight every Saturday night, began watching technique videos on YouTube when he was alone. Football became his still point, the way he made sense of the world.

After he accidentally broke his phone by stepping on it (it was under a pair of gym shorts) and couldn't watch drills on YouTube for a week, he started cleaning his room. He began doing his own laundry.

He had so much laundry due to all the workout clothes Mom had bought him. Mom seemed so proud of him. She actually watched him fold his laundry several times. "You're a different kid, aren't you?" she asked. He said yes. He said he was different. She bought him books about football, biographies of the greats, encyclopedias of terms, coaching books about different kinds of offenses he might face, about running 4–3 defense, 3–4, 4–2–5. He went to bed early, a book in hand. He got up early to work out.

And as long as he kept his schedule, his mind felt clear, and crisp. He felt like the new kid, the different Isaiah, the second Isaiah. But if he took even a day off, didn't read the books Mom gave him, didn't work out, his former dark thoughts would begin to emerge, and he'd feel that tiredness and sadness and he'd crave things (like the crazy stuff he did with Grace or a chemical buzz of another kind).

So, after a while, he stopped taking any days off. He began to see a future. There could be college? There could be an ensuing adulthood? No doubt football would be at the center of everything. It challenged his mind (learning all these high school, college, and pro defenses and committing to memory these hugely complex offenses). It exhausted him (a physically wiped Isaiah is a happy Isaiah). And most important, it thrilled him. Winning games with his teammates on the macro level. On the micro: big hits, turnovers, explosive plays that saved the day, that shot adrenaline through every part of him.

He made healthy breakfasts for himself every morning for those plays. He went to school for those plays. He went to bed for those plays. He lived for those plays.

He might be a thrill junkie. He might be an addict.

If he is, being a football addict is good. He stopped

looking for thrills off the field. His emotions were chan-
neled. His work habits spread into the classroom. He loved
his friends. He loved his parents, even as they continued
their post-Hannah disintegration. In fact, the more trouble
his parents had, the closer he got to Mom. Isaiah and Mom
stopped fighting. They began joking with each other, hav-
ing a movie night each Tuesday, planning trips they might
want to take. Mom took him over to Bluffton College to
meet with the coaches there. They run a decent Division III
program and were excited by the prospect of having a local
kid, a professor's kid (because Dad teaches engineering at
the college), a player of his talents and passion, who would
essentially have a free ride to the college due to his dad's
employment, in their recruiting sights. He didn't commit.
Dad wouldn't let him commit. But it was a commitment
in his mother's mind. That seemed okay to him. Why not
stay and play?

The football addiction gave him opportunities. It gave
him a belief in himself. It gave him peace in his house, even
after Dad abandoned the family. It gave him a future. . . .

It is definitely a good addiction.

We sat at a table in Joey's junky barn. We drank root beer
out of heavy glass mugs his grandpa used for real beer back in
the day.

Joey squinted at me. "Cool story, bro," he said. "So that's
how you got in with Riggles and Twine, huh? They actually

continue to be douchebags, you know? They're jerks to people."

"No. They're not. Not really. Not since sophomore year, probably. They're my best friends."

"What about me?"

"They're different from you."

"They sure are." He took a sip of his root beer. "Thrill junkie? It's hard to think of you like that. You're like the calmest dude I know."

"That's why football," I told him. "That's why. It keeps my problem in a healthy place."

"What's going to happen to you when you stop playing, like after your Hall of Fame pro career? Are you going to turn into a hitman or something? Maybe the government can turn you into a Jason Bourne biological cyborg murderer?"

"I'm too small to play pro," I said.

"How about this? What if you run weapons for the resistance?" he asked. "Do something honorable with all your pent-up violence?"

"I don't know. I really don't think about after football," I said. "I'm not ready to think about that."

"I'm going to think about it for you. You're in a jeep, cruising across the desert. You're wearing shades. A government helicopter suddenly flies up over a sand dune next to you. You stand up, steer with your feet. You leap into the sky, grab that chopper, and pull it down into the ground. *Boom!* You saved the resistance, dude!"

"What resistance?"

"THE resistance, dude. THE ONLY ONE!"

"Who are we resisting?"

"The forces of evil, man. Who else?"

Resisting the forces of evil. In a way, that made sense to me. Football helped me to resist my own evil inclinations. That was its primary role in my life.

That was before Cornell University offered me a scholarship.

CHAPTER

SEPTEMBER 30: AFTERNOON

Truth: I continued to feel like shit. After the Country Kitchen breakfast, I nearly threw up. I stayed lying on the bathroom floor in the basement for the better part of an hour after we got home. It was bad. And the plans I had for watching games and studying the rest of the day just couldn't happen. My broken bell meant bed was the only reasonable option.

I canceled my day by text. Grandma didn't respond (she received texts but never sent them). Dad asked, *Concussion?* I didn't reply. I told Twiggs I had the flu. Twiggs asked if I was okay after *that crazy hit.*

100 percent I responded, before turning off the lights in my room, pulling the curtains tight, and burying my head in the pillows.

I drifted into sleep. Back out. Had that conversation with Mom been real? It didn't seem real to me, sitting in Country Kitchen, the old people acting like synchronized swimmers, tilting their heads toward us in unison, trying to hear what? That I had to quit playing football? Mom said that, but it was impossible. Football was the future.

Really.

I had a big secret.

Our first game of the year had been against Glendale, a giant school in suburban Milwaukee. Given the school's size, Glendale thought they'd beat the crap out of us cornhole, small-town rubes (some names they called us). They barked at us across the field. They called us fat-ass farmers and hillbillies. They accused us of doing nasty things with farm animals. It's like they had no idea of who we were, even though we'd been kicking ass all over Wisconsin for a couple years.

I have to say, their nastiness pissed us off. We took it out on them. Five minutes in we'd knocked out their top running back and were up by two touchdowns. It was violent. I unloaded on that running back. They stopped talking shit. They looked like dogs with their tails between their legs.

By halftime we were up by twenty. By the final whistle, we'd destroyed Glendale, 40–14. And honestly, it could've been worse. Coach Reynolds sat our supertalented running back, Iggy, and our all-area quarterback, Riley, the whole fourth quarter. Twiggs, our all-conference split end, came out after one series in the fourth. I never came out—I told Coach Reynolds I wouldn't come out after we gave up two touchdowns at the end of a game sophomore year.

Yes, we destroyed Glendale. This was not a surprise, if you were paying attention. We'd unloaded on two giant suburban schools the year before, too.

There was a surprise, though. A serious recruiter had been there to see the Glendale quarterback. I had twelve tackles—violent tackles—a sack, a crazy, long bomb interception, and a fumble recovery that I returned for a touchdown. I, personally, had made that Glendale quarterback look like a middle schooler.

On my way off the field, this guy waited next to the stands. He wore a college insignia golf shirt, had big shoulders, and carried a clipboard. I knew he was a recruiter. I'd seen these dudes before but had mostly blown them off because I already knew what I was doing after high school—Bluffton College. The guy pulled me aside. Riley and Twiggs had gone into the locker room in front of me. Only a few underclassmen and scrubs walked behind. No one really saw the exchange.

"Isaiah Sadler?" the man said.

"Yeah?"

"You're a senior?"

"Yeah?"

"Have any D-I coaches come to see you play?"

"Last year. Wisconsin and Iowa State. They think I'm small, which is fine."

"You're not that small," the man said.

"No. I'm pretty small," I said.

"You're a baller, straight up. That's what I see."

I paused. Blinked. Looked at the red C with a bear climbing through it on the left chest of the dude's golf shit. "Who are you?" I asked.

"What kind of student are you, Isaiah?" the man asked. "Do you like school?"

"I don't know," I said. "But I'm second in my class. I probably should be first. My mom didn't want me to take AP Human Geography last year because it's tough and I had a lot of tough classes, so I got behind in AP credits. I'm taking it this year, though."

A big smile spread across the man's face. He reached out his hand to shake. "I'm Jim Conti. Cornell University."

"Cornell?" I said.

Since that game in mid-August, Conti had lit me up like the sun on a summer day. He texted several times a week. He called my cell once a week. He asked for my family's financial data. I broke the rules, went into Mom's office. I copied bank statements and tax returns from Mom's files. Conti asked for video, which I got from Kirby Sheldon, our team's student trainer and AV guy. That video showed again and again what Jim Conti saw in person, I suppose. Truth: I'm a little small. But, also, I am a baller, straight up. And based on my grades, my high ACT score, and, mostly, on my nose for the football, Cornell University, a great institution of higher learning—the alma mater of Supreme Court Justice Ruth Bader Ginsburg, and this writer I really like, Kurt Vonnegut, and Bill Nye the Science Guy, who Hannah and I watched on YouTube, and lots more (I googled everything about the school)—wanted to fly me out to Ithaca,

New York, to visit their campus. They were preparing to offer me a scholarship. . . .

But I hadn't told anybody else (except for Joey, who thought it was awesome). Coach Conti kept asking to talk to Mom or Dad. I made up excuses about how they were busy but were as excited about Cornell as I was. I'm not even sure what I was afraid of. Mom, I guess. How would she react if I told her I wanted to go back on the commitment I'd made to her to stay in Bluffton for college, to stay close to home, to keep our family together? That fear might seem stupid if there hadn't been all this death and disaster in my family.

Coach Conti texted Sunday around noon.

> Big win against Sacred Heart yesterday. Gave up too many points, though. We could use you out there! Harvard next week. When can we get you out here to see a game? Talk to your parents this week?

I shut my eyes tight. Slept the sleep of the dead, except I dreamed my recurring dream, which included Hannah drinking a black coffee at Badger Coffee on Main Street.

I woke. Twiggs texted again. Apparently, Aaron Rodgers threw a crazy touchdown to Davante Adams. I tried to focus on the phone screen, to see the highlight Twiggs sent. But I couldn't watch the motion. I couldn't track it. My eyes didn't work.

I am broken, I thought.

CHAPTER 10

THE DREAM

Early in September, I wrote about my recurring dream in my green notebook.

They are in Badger Coffee on Main Street in Bluffton. The walls are cherry red (not the coffee shop's real color). Hannah wears a red cardigan sweater (she never owned that piece of clothing in her life). All that red? For blood?

What does red mean in a dream?

(For the purpose of this story, I googled it—Sorry for the internet use, Joey.)

Red is an indication of raw energy, power, vigor, passion, force, courage, intensity, and impulsiveness.

Other than the red, Hannah is just Hannah. Not dead

but funny, sarcastic, pretty. They sit in the big window up front that looks out on the sidewalk. Isaiah is next to her. He's himself now, not the turbulent asshole kid he was back when she died. They're both drinking black coffee because they're not into a bunch of sugary bullshit. Their conversation feels normal until Isaiah remembers something's very wrong.

He turns to her and says, "Wait. What if I told you you're going to die tonight, Hannah?"

"I wouldn't believe you," she says.

"You wouldn't? But what if I'm right. What if I know you are? What if I know how? You'll be in Ray's Corolla."

"I like Ray's car. He keeps it clean. Dudes are usually so gross."

"You'll be out by Rewey."

"No way. We wouldn't go there."

"On the way back from Blackhawk Lake."

"Oh, maybe."

"You'll be going through an intersection."

"Hard to avoid that. Roads cross, don't they?"

"And you'll be creamed—like smeared, so your body is destroyed beyond recognition. A sad guy in a pickup truck will hit you."

"Wow, Isaiah. That's a little dark," she says, smiling.

"Don't smile."

This makes her smile harder.

"Will you still get in the car with Ray?"

"Tonight? No. I don't think so. I guess not. Not if you know for sure."

"Don't get in the car tonight, Hannah."

"I won't."

"Good call," Isaiah says.

"You just saved my life." Hannah laughs. Then she drinks her coffee. She looks out onto Main Street. An old lady walking with a cane is the only action out there. "What a boring piece-of-shit town," she says.

"But what about tomorrow?" Isaiah asks.

"What, I'm going to die tomorrow, too?"

"Yeah. Maybe. That pickup truck could be coming tomorrow."

Hannah turns from the window. She looks into Isaiah's eyes. Her eyes are so blue, like the sea in the movie Mamma Mia, which she watched a thousand times even though Isaiah complained about it. "Dude," she says. "That pickup could be coming every day for the rest of my life. You want me to stay in the house for the rest of my life?"

"Yes. Please?" Isaiah says.

"No," Hannah says. "No way!"

"But you never got a chance to live someplace else, Hannah. You never went to Greece! You never got married! You never sang songs with your friends in a bar!"

"It's okay, man," Hannah says. "Hey. Fill up your cup. You're empty."

Isaiah looks down at his empty cup. He nods. He goes

53

to get a refill. When he returns, Hannah is gone.

He runs out the door, spilling coffee, burning his hand.

Out by Rewey, Ray Gatos's car flies through an intersection. A half second later, a pickup truck screams through from the other direction. So close, but there is no crash. The truck barrels onward, whipping dust into horizontal tornadoes. Isaiah is left alone, standing on the gravel shoulder, watching both the truck and the car continue on their merry ways, getting farther apart, into the future, while the sun sets red and orange in Wisconsin's Driftless Area.

"Do the cars always miss at the intersection?" Joey asked after I read it to him.

"They never hit. But I know they're going to hit someday. I wake up sweating my ass off, my heart racing, because I thought they were going to hit. But they didn't. Don't. Not yet."

"We should go out there," he said. "Stand right where you're dreaming it. Pick up that energy. Don't you think?"

"No. I don't think so," I said. "I won't go there."

"You never have?"

"No. Never. Can't."

"You have to face it, bro. See it. Be with it."

I shook my head.

"It's just an intersection. Just like Hannah says in your dream. Roads cross."

"No," I said.

CHAPTER
11

OCTOBER 1: MONDAY

I got ready to go to school Monday, even though the world continued to be plastic and unreal. *Don't think,* I told myself. *Maybe this is a bad dream.*

"Are you going to meet with Coach Reynolds?" Mom asked before she left for work. "Do you need anything from me? Do you want me to come?"

"No," I said. "Thanks. I'll talk to him."

"I'm so sorry, Isaiah," Mom said. "I know this is going to be tough on you. Don't even think about the Bluffton College coaches. We can talk to them later. You're a strong kid and you're going to be okay."

"Okay," I said.

Okay? I had no plan for escaping this situation and definitely no plan to talk to any coach about my injury, about the doctor, about my mom, who thought she understood but, clearly, had no idea what she was doing to me. I prepared to go to school and tried to pretend it wasn't happening, because it couldn't be happening.

But I couldn't pretend with any measure of normalcy. The world was plastic? I wouldn't be playing in the game on Friday? Mom mentioned the Bluffton College coaches? What did that mean? I wouldn't be playing ever again?

Don't say anything to anyone about anything, my cracked brain said. *Inhabit your second life and this stupid sickness will go away.*

It was easy to act sick. I was sick. There was this weird weakness in my muscles. I was still groggy, unsteady. My sensitivity to sound and light was less than Sunday but still present. I kept shading my eyes, covering my ears. I texted Riley that I couldn't make weight lifting but would see him at school.

Because of that hit? Riley texted back.

No. Flu. Bad one. Puked yesterday. Recovering, I wrote.

I drove myself in Mom's Subaru (it was a nice day—she walked to her office when it was nice). Parked. Entered the school. Coming into the commons hurt badly, so much light and noise and action, four hundred high schoolers shouting across the room. I moved quickly, past all the people who talked at a volume that made my head vibrate.

I had to find a place to isolate, so I sat in a bathroom stall in the science hall for ten minutes before heading to my first-hour class. I felt so shitty in there, so I googled how many kids die from playing football each year. Not too many, was the answer. But, yeah, some. When first bell rang, I covered my ears, my eyes watered. Then I got up and made myself move into the bright hallway toward class, physics.

Riley and Twiggs were both there. Twiggs was jacked up that we hadn't gotten together the night before. I sat down in my seat.

"Dude. I couldn't even start the assignment. No clue. We were going to go over it at your dad's last night, remember? I couldn't do the shit without you. There's my first zero."

I'd finished it the Thursday before. "Sorry, man. I'm pretty sick."

"Why are you here if you're sick, man?" Riley asked.

"Don't like missing."

"Huh." Riley stared at me, thinking. "When did you get sick? Did you puke right after the game?" he asked.

"No. More in the morning. Saturday morning," I said.

"What's wrong with your voice?" Twiggs asked. "You're mumbling."

"Could be a concussion," Riley said. "I fell off a snowmobile in sixth grade and got my bell rung, bad. I puked ten times. It was ugly."

"No," I said. "No concussion, just a flu."

Tyra Ramirez, who sits on the other side of me, pulled her sweatshirt over the lower part of her face. "Keep your disease to yourself, Isaiah."

I pulled my T-shirt over the lower half of my face. "Sorry," I said.

"You have to rest up, man," Twiggs said. "I once had the flu for a month."

"Flu doesn't last a month!" Tyra said. "But maybe a week. I can't be sick for a week! I got tests!"

"You should go home, Isaiah. Do you want the whole team to get sick?" Riley asked.

I hadn't thought of that. Coming to school with my "flu" wasn't good for other people. I shut my eyes. The stupid school lighting was so bright.

Then Mr. Urness, the physics teacher, turned the lights off and on. That made my head ring. I could see the firing light through my closed eyes. The classroom fell silent around me. "Happy Monday," he said.

The class groaned. I opened my eyes.

"Do any of you remember last week?" Mr. Urness asked.

Twiggs raised his hand. "I don't."

"What about this?" Mr. Urness asked. "Energy can neither be created nor destroyed. It only changes form. Anyone know what I'm talking about?"

The class was silent until Twiggs repeated, "I don't."

Energy cannot be created or destroyed?

Mr. Urness looked at me. "Mr. Sadler," he said, "to what am I referring?"

Bright light. People staring. My brain struggled to make a coherent sound over the noise of the bells ringing, but something fell out of my mouth. "Energy can't be created. It can't be destroyed. It only changes form. That's the first law of thermo-dynamics."

"Right. It's the law," Urness said.

"My boy is wicked smart," Twiggs said.

"Energy changes form," I said.

"Mumble to yourself much?" Tyra asked.

"Energy cannot be extinguished," Mr. Urness said.

Hannah. Her energy cannot be destroyed. Her energy changes form. What did it change into? Where did it go? Did it hang together as Hannah's specific energy? A ghost Hannah? Did it disperse into the ground, into trees, into clouds, into rain? Did it become part of everything?

The room began to spin and swoop. I covered my ears. Mr. Urness put up a PowerPoint. I covered my eyes, which exposed my ears. I thought I was going to get sick on my desk.

I raised my hand. "I'm really sick," I said.

"You don't sound like yourself," Mr. Urness said.

Five minutes into first hour, I got a pass and went back home to sleep.

Not normal. Not my second life. In fact, I think this was the end of my second life.

The day collapsed into noise and light and nightmares and bed spins.

"Did you talk to Coach Reynolds before you left?" Mom asked in the evening.

"I made an appointment to discuss it," I said. "But had to come home, you know?"

"I know, sweetheart," Mom said. She stroked my head, which hurt, but I didn't tell her to stop.

CHAPTER 12

THE ICE BOWL

Isaiah Sadler was only born because of a specific team and a specific moment in the history of American football.

Cue the dramatic music.

Nobody in his family ever played the sport, but he still grew up in the culture of the sport, from babyhood on. He watched the NFL with Grandma Gin, Grandpa John, Dad, Mom, sometimes Melinda (Mom's sister), and whoever was Melinda's romantic partner at the time, a woman for many years, which did not seem to bother Grandma Gin or Grandpa John—but then a man, Tom, who she married. Hannah was there on the floor with coloring books and crayons.

The family room at Grandma Gin's is a shrine to the

Green Bay Packers. There are framed posters of legendary coach Vince Lombardi, quarterback Bart Starr, defensive end Reggie White ("He was such a nice man"), and Grandma's favorite player of all, the cocksure, grinning quarterback with the rocket arm, Brett Favre. In two glass cases on either side of the big TV, there are signed footballs, commemorative placards, player action figures, and frames filled with sixty years of team trading cards. Dozens of Packer yearbooks line a bookshelf. A golden vase contains two miniature flags, which bloom like flowers: the Packer G flag and old glory herself, the Stars and Stripes. There are green and gold beanbag chairs for the kids (one kid gone, one too big to sit there anymore). There are a brown leather couch and recliner and a worn out green-and-gold recliner that used to be Grandpa John's but is Grandma's chair now.

If you ask Isaiah he will tell you: This is where I come from.

In truth, he would almost surely not exist if not for the Green Bay Packers.

Why? On December 31, 1967, the Wisconsin State–La Crosse marching band was set to perform before the NFL Championship Game in Green Bay, Wisconsin. Grandma Gin, then a scant freshman, twirled baton for the band. The game was a huge deal. She couldn't believe her luck. She couldn't believe she got to attend. The winner (Packers versus Cowboys) would go on to play in the second Super Bowl ever held.

Incredible. Poor kid from the western hills gets to see this game? Gin hadn't been sure about college—she wanted to earn money more than anything, not read books. But then, twirling batons got her to Lambeau Field? What an opportunity!

Except, it was cold outside. Incredibly cold.

Green Bay Packer cornerback Willie Wood couldn't start his car that morning. It was frozen shut. He told the tow truck guy, "No way we play a game today. No way. It's too cold."

Frank Gifford, CBS color commentator, sat in the broadcast booth before the game. He stared down at what had just moments earlier been a steaming mug. "Let me take a bite out of my coffee," he said. The coffee had frozen solid.

The marching band rolled up to the historic stadium and unloaded their equipment. They shivered and shook as they did so. A nasty wind ripped through their uniforms, especially the flag girls and baton twirlers, who were asked to wear skirts in all weather. They were already cold when they arrived! The heaters on the bus that brought them couldn't deal with wind chills of forty degrees below zero.

Many band members began to grumble.

"Maybe we should throw in the towel?"

"This is too much."

"No one is going to sit in the stands to watch us in this stupid weather."

Gin got nervous. Would the Packers still let them watch the game if they didn't march?

As a band, they decided to delay making the decision to cancel. These were all Wisconsin kids. When would they get this opportunity again?

They made their way through the entrance tunnel and to the field, where they saw a grounds crew in panic mode. The band hung back and watched as men wearing thick golden coats tried to get feeble heaters to blow across the field.

It turned out that the heaters on the bus weren't the only ones that couldn't deal with that kind of cold. The subterranean heating coils—the ones that usually kept the Lambeau Field turf feeling like Kentucky bluegrass in the springtime—had also malfunctioned, shut down. And when the grounds crew removed the giant tarp covering the field, a thin layer of moisture, which had built up under the tarp, flash froze, turning the turf into a carpet of icy razor blades. The band waited and waited. Finally, a crew manager came up and said, "You can get out there and see, but I wouldn't recommend it."

"Let's just take a look," said one baritone horn player. So, the band stumbled onto the field to see if there was any possibility. And when they did, something miraculous happened. A giant, wild, drunken crowd cheered like crazy. "It sounded so odd," Gin said. "Like fifty-thousand seals got together for an outdoor rock-and-roll concert on an iceberg."

Yes. Fifty-thousand Green Bay Packers fans were already there—the whole mass of them buried under wool blankets, snowmobile suits, and ice fishing gloves pulled up to their elbows. They braved deadly temperatures and packed the stadium, ready to cheer on their home-town heroes, even if they might die doing so. Their breath turned instantly to steam when they shouted, shrouding the entirety of the stadium in roiling silver clouds.

"It was those thick mittens that made the funny noise. Seals in heat. That's what they sounded like," Gin said.

That baritone player, a large man named John Bertram, a good-looking fellow, even if he had a square head, stood up in front of the rest of the band and said, "If these fans can muster the courage to cheer out here, can't us God-dang college kids muster the piss and brandy to perform for them?"

The band answered yes. Emphatically.

And so, a couple minutes later they whipped off their heavy coats, and marched onto the frozen field, ready to perform the pregame show, to play a tribute to the circus called "The Greatest Show on Earth."

Have you ever seen the "Triple Dog Dare" part of the movie A Christmas Story? *On a dare, a kid flash freezes his tongue to a frozen light post and the police and fire depart-ment are called to extract him. Imagine that scene, but a lot bigger, a whole marching band placing frozen instru-ments made either entirely from metal, or containing* metal parts, into their mouths. . . .

That baritone player, John Bertram, was the first to notice his face was frozen to his instrument. Out of shock, he dropped the baritone, which was a bad move, because when he dropped it, half his upper lip came off on the mouthpiece. He cried out in pain.

The trouble spread. Woodwind reeds splintered, cutting the tongues of clarinetists. Saxophonists found their fingers spit-glued to their instruments. Mylar drumheads shattered, firing frozen plastic into the faces of drummers. Flag girls' flagpoles broke. And the wind whipped broken blades of razor grass across the bare legs and ankles of the baton twirlers. Gin lost at least a half gallon of blood, which froze to her flesh, turning her legs dark red.

The cataclysm was so quick, no one in the stands understood what was happening. They stopped their seal clapping and looked on confused, because the band, including the drummers, stopped playing right as they'd started. Some marchers fell to the ground. Some stumbled off the field dazed and confused.

One man got it, though. Pat Summerall, a sideline reporter for CBS Sports. He was close enough to see there were serious weather-related injuries afoot. He signaled the booth, called out instructions into his headset, and soon ambulances arrived on the field to pick up marching band casualties.

Seven band members were taken to local hospitals,

others were taken deep into the warm bowels of the stadium for treatment.

Gin, although she lost a lot of blood, chose to skip medical treatment. She was inspired once again by the baritone player, John Bertram. He had shoved medical staff away from him. He had shouted that they'd have to cut off his whole head to keep him from staying and cheering for his beloved Green Bay Packers. Gin didn't really know him yet—John Bertram was a junior—but when she saw him fight like a junkyard dog to stay, even though he had just lost his upper lip, she thought to herself, "I will marry that crazy bastard."

And that's what she did. One year later they both dropped out of college and John Bertram became Grandpa John and Gin Weissman became Grandma Gin Bertram.

The Packers wouldn't let down their fans, either. They won that game, the famous "Ice Bowl," in the final minute. Bart Starr's winning quarterback sneak (including the roiling silver clouds emanating from the fans in the stands) would be replayed a billion times on television (and now on YouTube). The Packers fought through bone-cracking cold, stayed together, beat the mighty Cowboys, and found themselves headed out to the Super Bowl, in the much warmer confines of the Orange Bowl Stadium, in Miami, Florida. They went filled with Wisconsin courage, carrying with them the values of optimism, grit, and excellence. Those are American values, Grandpa John would say. The

Green Bay Packers won that Super Bowl.

John Bertram's values. He dropped out of college because he couldn't abide by his collegiate deferment from Vietnam. "All those Black boys and poor boys get sent off while I sit here in a classroom? That isn't right. That can't be right." He went over there. He did a tour and a half. Got shot in his thigh and came home with a bunch of medals for valor. The bullet didn't stop him from going to where the danger was again, from becoming a cop, then a detective, then working for the Wisconsin Bureau of Criminal Apprehension, and even helping out on an investigation after he retired, which got him shot dead on a country road.

He was a good dude. Grandma Gin was a good person. While Grandpa fought crime, she opened the Dairy Queen. She worked hard and believed in the rightness of what she did. She said she was always happy. "Never had a dark day until John died." They loved their kids, and accepted and loved their lesbian daughter, Melinda, and accepted her decision to marry a man later. They accepted and loved the Jewish man Dan who married their daughter Tammy (even though he was a New York Giants fan!). Isaiah saw the way other people in his small town sometimes treated people who were different from themselves. He knew his own grandparents were different, better, bigger hearted than all those others. He loved them for it.

But know this: If not for the Ice Bowl, Isaiah's grandmother wouldn't have known John Bertram's giant heart,

*and she would never have married him and then Isaiah's
mother would never have been born and so Isaiah would
never have been born.*

To this legendary game he owes his existence.

So did Hannah.

*But Hannah was gone and Grandpa John was gone and
then Melinda got divorced and Grandma Gin began to say
nasty things, disheartening things, to Melinda about the
way Melinda lived her life, which made Melinda stay away
and so it felt like Melinda was gone and Dan and Tammy
didn't recover from Hannah dying, so their marriage was
gone, but for some reason, those who lived showed up for
Isaiah's football games (even Melinda several times). They
sat in the stands together and cheered. They were nice to
each other up there.*

*Isaiah kept them together. Dan (Dad), Tammy (Mom),
Melinda (Aunt), Gin (Grandma). Because he played football?*

At least he kept them talking.

Yes. He believed that.

"You know, bro, you're sort of a narcissist, right?" Joey said.

"Why? Are you kidding?" I asked.

"Do you really think you matter so much? Or your grandpa
mattered so much? Do you really think you're part of Green
Bay Packer lore?"

"Oh," I said. "I don't know."

"Do you really think you matter so damn much to your mom? Like, if you went away she'd die or something?"

"I think she would die if I died," I said.

"Let go of yourself so you can be yourself," Joey said.

"Where do you come up with this stuff?" I asked.

"I read that on a poster up at Spencer's in the mall in Dubuque," he said.

CHAPTER 13

OCTOBER 2: TUESDAY

On Tuesday morning, I felt better. Legitimately. My head on a pillow for almost twenty hours straight (with trips to the bathroom and two cups of tea in between) actually helped.

When I turned on my bedside lamp at 6:45, the light didn't bother me much. That was a first since Friday. The sound of Mom's electric toothbrush in the bathroom as I walked down the hall didn't chase me back to bed, either. I stood at the counter, drank a cup of coffee, ate three hard-boiled eggs, and looked at my phone to see what assignments were due (and I could read my screen). And then realized I'd totally fallen behind because I hadn't done a minute of homework since last Thursday.

Mom walked in, wearing her business dress. "You have your

meeting with Coach Reynolds today? It's going to be tough. But it's the right thing, you know?"

I sighed. "Mom," I said, leaning on the refrigerator, "how about I stay home?"

"You still dizzy?" She pressed her cold hand against my forehead. "Not better than yesterday? Should we go back to the doctor? What if you're bleeding internally or something?"

"No. I feel good, actually. Really good. Normal."

"Don't lie."

To show my improvement, I said, "Look, okay?" I did three jumping jacks. "I'm not dizzy. See? No dizziness."

"Okay? So? School?"

"I got behind on homework. Need a catch-up day."

"You're not just avoiding having a hard discussion, are you? Do you want me to call Coach Reynolds? I'm serious, Isaiah. We can go in together."

"Jesus. I just need to get my damn homework done," I spat. "I'm not a third grader."

I never shouted at Mom. She took a step back. "Do what you think is right, kid," she said. "But you owe it to your teammates to let them know. They're going to have to adjust to this as much as you are."

"I have to catch up on homework," I said.

"Fine," she said. She softened. "You're going to be okay, okay?"

"Okay," I said.

"Call me if you need anything."

Mom would never have let Hannah have a catch-up day, but she was a different human being now. Dad often complained that she coddled me. Mom often told Dad to stay in his lane. If he hadn't left us, maybe he could have a say sometimes. In this situation? Had she even talked to Dad about it? What would he say about me quitting football?

I didn't want to know. He's not an idiot. He'd probably agree.

I stayed home, drank water, did schoolwork, felt physically better. Did not think about Mom or football. Around noon, I made myself tomato soup and a grilled cheese while singing along to the '90s Pandora station Mom kept up on her desktop computer in the living room. Half those old bands are impossible to understand when they sing, but I sang anyway.

Life crept back into the universe. Heated the plastic and made it malleable. Chased dust, sand, cobwebs away. It felt good to be inside myself. Singing (I'm a shit singer). Feeling the emotion of the music. Because those old '90s songs are filled with real feeling, even if the words make no damn sense. My soul was inside my body. I could feel it.

Then, while I was washing the lunch dishes, I looked out the back window toward Grandma's house. Things weren't right out there. Not at all. Things were out of place. A pointy girl stood on Grandma's deck. Pointy girl. Grace. My Grace (yes, my Grace, even though I hadn't talked to her in almost two years). She smoked a cigarette like she did in half my memories of her. She looked in my direction. Could she see me in the window staring out at her like some frozen gazelle facing a lioness?

I dropped out of sight. I slid to lying on the floor. What was Grace doing at Grandma's house?

Grace. My Grace. Why? Hanging out with Grandma? Doing Dairy Queen business with Grandma? Grace was the store manager. But wouldn't Grace and Grandma do their business at Dairy Queen, not at the house in my backyard? What business, anyway? Blizzards? Nobody makes Blizzards in their own house. No way. Or . . . maybe Grace was robbing Grandma, selling Grandma's jewelry for drug money? Murdering Grandma for drug money . . .

Oh, come on. . . .

Maybe she was dropping something off—paperwork, tax forms, time cards (which are all done on the computer and could be sent by email)—and then decided to stand in the backyard to smoke her cigarette . . . or . . .

What if she missed me? Just wanted to see my house? Wanted to remember being with me. Remember when we were together, secretly. She couldn't know I'd be home in the middle of the day. What if she missed me?

I missed her.

Shit. I shut my eyes.

Grace.

CHAPTER 14

GRACE

"I've been thinking about love and my general lack of romance, lately," Joey said while we were up on ladders, pulling years of leaves and assorted debris from Barb Larson's gutters. "There aren't many possible partners out there for me, bro. I'm way ahead of my time, you know? I'm a wise old man in a glowing and beautiful newbie's body. What a waste of temple space." Joey happened to be shirtless (he worked without a shirt all summer, which just turned his bony white chest pink). He pointed at himself. "Look at my beauty, dude. I'm a hot young slice of bacon, am I not?"

"I know," I said. "You're a sexy temple."

"Waste." He shook his head. "I bet I get plenty of love when I'm, like, forty, though."

"Probably. Can't wait. We'll double-date."

"You? You won't find love, bro. I mean, when's the last time you had girlfriend or a boyfriend?"

"You know the answer to that."

"Right. Your mom is your girlfriend."

"Dude. Stop. Twiggs and Riley keep saying that crap and it's starting to piss me off."

"You don't get pissed. You probably smile and laugh, like it doesn't bother you that they perceive the vicious truth about you and your mom girlfriend."

"Seriously. Stop."

"It's pretty gross, though, bro." Joey laughed.

"I don't have room. I'm not over Grace."

"Oh, Bonnie? You miss her, Clyde? Can't find another suitable partner in crime?"

"I don't want another partner in crime," I said. "I just like Grace."

"What do you want? I'll get you a Tinder profile. Let's get you out on the love market."

"No. Just her," I said. "Only her."

"Dude. That's effed. She's just Grace, some townie screwup like every other kid here. Why the hell is she such a big deal?"

I thought for a second. "I don't really know," I said.

"Green notebook, you big-brained ape," Joey said. "Search your feelings, Luke."

"Thanks. I will, Yoda."

"Darth Vader said that, man! It's like you don't know your bible at all!"

He'd crushed on her from the moment she went to work for Grandma. That was right before Hannah died. He and Grace hooked up for the first time six months after Hannah, when Grace had just turned sixteen and he was fourteen. They'd been closing Dairy Queen all winter together, just the two of them.

Part of the deal Grandma had made with Grace was that Grace had to give little grandson, Isaiah, a ride home after they finished each shift, which meant their nights together could go on and on. Isaiah was a messed-up kid. Grace was in control of his time.

Which was fine with him. Isaiah and Grace got along really well. Like, too well. Like, they were one person with one deviant brain. At some point, she started pouring her mom's vodka into a water bottle and bringing it with her so they could get buzzed while they cleaned. Then, one night, they kissed. The next they made out. Then they got buzzed and messed around every single night.

Grace was always such a worker, though, so thorough, it still looked like they were doing a good job. She was a functioning addict.

Isaiah wanted to brag to his dipshit friends, Reid and Ben, about her, but Grace told him if he told anyone she would never speak to him again. He listened. She was an older girl and her presence in his life promised all this incredible pleasure, which he needed. His mom was wrecked back then, still crying for Hannah every day. His dad, who had been hilarious, gregarious, had gone totally silent for Hannah. Grandma Gin hadn't recovered from the loss of Grandpa John. No one seemed to care that Isaiah was in danger of flunking out of eighth grade or going to jail—he was already seeing a court-ordered social worker after getting busted for burning Christmas trees in Smith Park, for God's sake! No way he would go against anything Grace said. He needed her so much. To her, he could say he dreamed of his sister, Hannah, opening presents under the Christmas tree, riding her bike super fast on the street in front of their house, playing the board game Sorry! with Isaiah and Grandpa. Grace would listen. Grace would hug him. Grace would say, "It's cool you liked Hannah so much. She was pretty awesome. I know it." Grace was the only person on the planet who looked at him, listened to him, and smiled at him.

She didn't seem to need him at all but kept coming back to him again and again. So, she probably really did need him, but . . .

In April, she agreed to go to prom with a kid named Caleb Wilson, who used to come over to Isaiah's house to study with Hannah. Isaiah wanted to beat Caleb up, maybe kill him, but he didn't do anything, because he needed Grace to like him. Then, after prom, Grace decided she liked Caleb enough to call him her boyfriend. It killed Isaiah, made him retch in the bathroom. Repeatedly.

Maybe Isaiah would've gotten over it, but Grace didn't

cut him off. She kept messing with him, bringing vodka for him, making out with him at the end of shifts, but being mean to him right after, sometimes screaming at him. She stopped wanting to hear about how he missed Hannah. She'd say, "I can't deal with your ghost world right now."

Isaiah felt sick all the time. He broke the driver's side mirror off Caleb Wilson's car one night. Then, in May, Grace's estranged stepfather moved back into their house and Grace made Isaiah hide a bottle of vodka.

"I can't hide it in my room. Richie will find it. He comes in, digs through my shit all the time."

"I don't want it," Isaiah said. "You want my mom to find it? Keep it in your car."

"Caleb might find it in my car. He'll break up with me. You know what my grade is like."

Isaiah did know. The smart kids in Grace's class were all militant against alcohol, because of what happened to Ray Gatos and Hannah. They joined FOCUS, DARE, SADD. They signed pacts saying they'd never drink.

"I hope Caleb breaks up with you," Isaiah said. "It would be good for him if he broke up with you."

"Come on," she whispered in his ear. "Please? Just hide the bottle. You can have some." So, Isaiah took the bottle home.

Three days later he found out Grace was going with Caleb's family on a trip to Chicago. The following day Isaiah's parents went to Dubuque for a marriage therapy session. While they were gone, Isaiah drank what was left of the vodka (a half liter) and he nearly died (after breaking all this shit in his own kitchen, not Caleb's). Dad found him naked, bleeding, passed out on the floor of the basement shower. Isaiah got a trip to the emergency room. There, his social worker suggested he spend time at a dry group home.

Grace had troubles, but she was very good at hiding her troubles. Isaiah was not good at hiding his trouble at all.

He continued to love Grace, even though she was the source of more trouble. Mom tried to pry out of him where the booze had come from, but Isaiah would not tell.

In fact, nobody would've known about Grace's hand in his demise if she hadn't confessed her sins to Mom a few years later, when Isaiah was a sophomore in high school. This confession was part of Grace's AA program.

Mom was not nice about it. Mom lost her mind. She wanted to hire a lawyer. Press charges.

"Press what charges?" Isaiah asked. "Aiding and abetting my teenaged delinquency while being a teenager?"

Mom asked Grandma to fire Grace. But Grandma wouldn't.

"She's my best worker and she needs my help."

Mom refused to let Isaiah ever work at Dairy Queen again. Mom wrote nasty things about Grace on Facebook (without using Grace's name, but all the townies on Facebook knew). But the truth is, Mom didn't know even the beginning about him and Grace. Even after football, after he got clean, he'd sometimes meet with her, drive out to *the Belmont Tower with her, climb up to the top, where they could be alone. They talked, mostly. Grace knew the real Isaiah better than just about anyone.*

So Isaiah had these feelings for Grace. They wouldn't go away.

Back during the summer after eighth grade, when she was "dating" Caleb and he got sent away to a group home, he felt addicted to her like a drug. In fact, the first four weeks he was in the home (between fistfights and smoke breaks), Isaiah writhed from missing Grace. He couldn't sleep at night. His insides longed for her. He considered killing himself to get her attention. When the social workers gave him his phone (one hour every night), he texted her. He called her. He left pleading messages. She responded with a one-word text, Relax. *He texted,* What if I die? *She responded,* Just don't. *But he really thought he might die.*

Thankfully he went to group counseling every day. During week four, he spoke about Grace in counseling. He spoke about Mom and about Hannah and about Dad. The counselors listened. Some of the other dudes his age listened. They all talked. Gave him advice. He started thinking that maybe he was trying to replace Hannah with Grace and that was weird as hell and it could only be a bad scene. Grace wasn't his family. She was just a girl he met at work. He began to let her go. Tried so hard. Then Mom decided to bring him home, because he'd somehow managed to pass eighth grade and high school would be a new start for him. For all of them. She missed him. She needed to have her baby home. . . .

When Isaiah returned at the end of July, he tried to stay away from Grace, because he understood their relationship was bad for him.

The family made him go back to work at Dairy Queen, though. This was long before Grace confessed, so no one else knew. The family thought work would keep him grounded. "Can't hang out with those idiots Ben and Reid if you're cleaning Dairy Queen bathrooms," Dad had said.

Bad move. Grace wouldn't stay away from him. She and Caleb had broken up. The breakup was because she missed Isaiah, she said. She realized that Caleb couldn't replace Isaiah, didn't hold a candle to Isaiah. She never even really liked Caleb, had only wanted to be with someone in her own grade.

And Isaiah just couldn't deal. The daily group counseling he received in Muscoda didn't give him the structure he needed to handle her. One night Grace cornered him by the dumpster behind the store. She cried, like really sobbed. She said she didn't have anyone in the world to talk to and she needed to be with someone who liked her—everybody hated her—and now she'd even made Isaiah hate her.

"I don't hate you. I would never hate you," Isaiah said.

"Thanks, man," she cried. "Thank you."

They hugged. Isaiah felt like he'd come home.

Two nights later, they closed the store together. Although

Isaiah was hesitant, he accompanied Grace to a corn-field keg party in a nearby town. The party was busted by county sheriffs. Isaiah was hauled to jail with a dozen other kids. The next day, his dad gave him the ultimatum. Play football or go back to Muscoda. Muscoda seemed like the right choice. Isaiah felt safe in Muscoda. But Dad gave him football and football gave him structure, a place, an identity, a reason. And so, here he is, a football player who doesn't work at Dairy Queen and doesn't ever talk to the love of his life.

"Ha," Joey said after he read that in my green notebook. "Come on! You're eighteen, bro. Love of your life? You don't know who the love of your life is." We were sitting at Badger Coffee, supposedly planning out how much paint we'd need to cover a shed in Potosi.

"I'm not eighteen. Not until October. And I don't care. I want Grace or no one and I'm not going to be with Grace, so I only play football."

"Football! Football! You're into monoculture!"

"Mono what?" I asked. "What the hell?"

"Okay. Listen. Like in farming? Monoculture is efficient. If you're a farmer? Only grow corn, bro. That's simple, cheap. Only need certain equipment and chemicals and whatnot. But what happens if a plague of corn-eating grasshoppers comes for your crops? You have nothing else to eat or sell at the market?"

"You're comparing me to a farmer?"

"No. You could be a factory town. Coal-mining town. Farming town. Doesn't matter. Each based on a single damn industry. They boom when times are good, but when things change, they die. Ghost town. Spiders and cobwebs and crooked tombstones by the empty church, right? All because they placed a bet on a single damn way of being. Wrong choice! Places need polyculture to protect themselves from change. Places need a diversified economic base, dude. Corn price goes to shit? Corn dies from too much rain? No worries. We have beans and cows and ham sandwiches. We have so much life! Our tombstones will be taken care of! Point is, without football, you've got no life, Isaiah. So you see ghosts. Hannah and Grace, right?"

"How much paint do we need to paint that damn shed?" I asked.

Back home, my day off to catch up on homework, I lay on the kitchen floor. Grace smoked a cigarette a backyard away from me? Right now?

What if this nightmare doesn't die? I wondered. What if Mom called Coach Reynolds today without telling me? What if football-eating grasshoppers are coming for my football crop?

If that happened, my energy wouldn't be destroyed. It would have to be transformed.

Maybe you should go talk to Grace, I said to myself.

I stood up, looked out the window.

She was gone.

CHAPTER 15

OCTOBER 3: WEDNESDAY

By Wednesday morning, I was caught up with schoolwork. Other than being rocked by the sight of Grace, the day before had been okay. If someone asked, I'd have said, "No, sir. No dizziness. No headaches. No sensitivity to light or sounds." I would not have mentioned Grace smoking a cigarette at Grandma's. I would not have mentioned me falling onto the floor and lying there for fifteen minutes. I would not have mentioned football-eating grasshoppers and the fate of tombstones in ghost towns.

So as not to set off any alarm bells, I texted Riley and took a ride in for weight lifting. I couldn't tell him the doctor said no working out of any kind. I couldn't tell him the thought of working out remained unappealing. So, once there, I claimed I needed to stretch instead of lift, because my illness had left me feeling tight and in danger of straining a muscle.

"What?" Riley said. "Stretching isn't a workout."

"Some forms of yoga are aerobic," I said.

"Are you going to do yoga? Did your mom teach you yoga now?"

"No, dude. I'm just tight. Give me a break. Yoga is dumb."

I don't really think yoga is dumb. Mom does it and it helps her with sciatica pain.

I went to stretch by myself. After, Riley asked if I wanted to leave during lunch, to grab a sandwich at Subway.

"I'm pretty behind on schoolwork," I said. The idea of having a conversation did not appeal to me. At lunch, we'd talk about the River Valley game. We'd probably talk about the bigger game, Prairie du Chien, coming up a week later. We might talk about other teams in the state doing well, teams we might meet in the playoffs. We might talk about college. Minnesota State and Northern Iowa were recruiting Riley hard. Coach Conti from Cornell had texted me the night before, had asked when was a good time to have a phone call with my parents, and I hadn't responded. If Riley mentioned any of these topics, I would freeze. I couldn't deal with that possibility. "I'm going to head to the library for lunch, I guess," I said.

"Aw, come on, dude," Riley said. "You're going to get into college. You're fine."

"I haven't done the reading assignment for Human Geography," I said.

"I did it," Riley said. "Here. Listen. I'll tell you all about it. You know why New York City has so many people all living on top of each other like rats? It developed before cars. They couldn't get too far away from their jobs so they had to pile on top of each other. That got easier when elevators were invented. Then they piled way up high in the sky. Make sense? Everybody had to be in walking distance from everything, okay?"

"Yeah. Thanks."

"No. Come on. Northern Iowa called me last night. I'm going to visit, man. I want to talk to you about it. Twiggs just says, 'Duuude, awesome.' Northern Iowa is D-I! Maybe they'd want to talk to you, too?"

"Jesus. I said I have to read," I spat.

Riley's face turned red. "What the hell is wrong with you?" he asked.

"Sorry. I'm stressed. From being sick. And school. Sorry."

"Whatever," Riley said. He walked away.

The rest of Wednesday was not okay.

There were times during different class periods where my mind wandered or shut down. I got the cold sweats a few times. I felt a little dizzy and nauseous. I thought about Cornell. I thought about Northern Iowa. I thought about my mom and Coach Reynolds. I thought about losing my life. I thought about Grace in my backyard and about her and me up at Belmont Tower alone.

By the end of the day, I was exhausted. And then, I realized, I had to go to football practice if I was going to pretend it all wasn't happening, to give me more time to work things out. It somehow only occurred to me at that moment—in Human Geography, trying to stay awake through a movie about shantytowns in South America—that I'd have to tell the coaches something, because I couldn't actually practice. My body didn't want me to practice. I couldn't go home sweaty, even if I was okay—Mom would lose her mind if I participated in football. And the doctor said I had to take the week off. . . .

My head was legitimately injured. My brain, injured. I was losing myself. My life.

Nobody, outside of me, the doctor, Mom, and Dad knew anything about anything.

Why wasn't I fighting Mom about making me quit? Why wasn't I telling people about my injury? What was happening to me?

For the first time, I got legitimately scared. My brain really couldn't be functioning right, even if I couldn't feel it malfunctioning, exactly. I had no excuse for sitting out of practice. Not just Wednesday but Thursday, too. What would I say about the game Friday? What was I going to do about what came after? How could I hide from this terrible thing happening in my life? I couldn't face it. I couldn't deal. I began to feel panic rising in my chest.

I put my head down on my desk and exhaled. I think I started crying into my sleeve.

Ms. Ross, the Human Geography teacher, came over and whispered in my ear. "Wake up, Isaiah."

CHAPTER 16

OCTOBER 3: WEDNESDAY AFTER SCHOOL

"I'm too ill to practice," I said to Coach Reynolds.

He sat behind a big metal desk that had probably been in this particular coaches' office since Mom graced the halls of Bluffton High School. "Ill how?" he asked. "What is making you so sick? You haven't been at practice all week."

"Flu, I guess," I said.

"Flu? You go to the doctor? You know it's flu, Sadler?" he asked.

"No. I haven't gone to a doctor."

"If you're this sick, you better see a doctor. You need to get on meds, you know? You got to take care of yourself. Your health isn't a joke."

"Okay," I said. "Maybe I'll go to the doctor now?"

"Urgent care," he said, nodding. "Do that. Get some meds. We need you back on the field, bud. You know that."

"Yeah," I said. "I know."

I am a liar. I really am. It might be one of my defining characteristics. I've known this for a long time. I tell people what they want to hear because I want them to be happy, or to like me, or maybe just not to know the real me. It doesn't come from nowhere. What I did when I was in eighth grade traumatized me as much as it did Mom and Dad. I don't want to cause people to suffer anymore. So, I don't tell the truth.

Instead of going to the doctor's office, I drove to Dairy Queen. Maybe to get a Blizzard?

Probably to see if Grace was there.

Yes. That's what I did. I went to Dairy Queen to see Grace—visually, not that I wanted to interact with her. I wanted to see her. That's all.

Here's me not being myself to make people happy. Sophomore year, right after I got my license, Grace and I had begun hanging out again. We'd begun secretly going to movies in Dubuque together and going up Belmont Tower late at night to talk about stuff and sometimes I'd climb the back porch of her house and slide over the roof and into her bedroom window after her mom had drunk herself to sleep on the couch downstairs.

It was good for me. Grace is my second home. That's what she felt like. I could be myself with Grace, which made it easier to be "stand-up" Isaiah for Mom.

But Grace wasn't in good shape. She didn't go to parties, but drank in small doses all day long. She'd pretty much stopped going to school. Her stepdad kept coming back and leaving and breaking stuff and begging her mom for forgiveness and there was something else with him, too, something worse, something between him and Grace.

In early November of that year, she wrecked her car after she closed the store, hit a parked car two blocks from home, left the scene of the accident, was arrested at her house the next day. There was no alcohol in her system by that time, but I know she was drunk. No doubt. Although the cops couldn't prove it, they thought so, too. She got to choose between giant fines, jail time, and alcohol awareness classes. She chose the last option (as any sane person would), and I'm glad she did, because I know from Grandma Gin that Grace doesn't drink anymore. Except those classes led her to another program and that program led to our final end.

She was in Alcoholics Anonymous. Part of that program was apologizing to those she'd harmed, making amends. She'd already apologized to me, even though I didn't need any apology. And even though I told her not to, begged her not to do it, she went to Mom. Grace told Mom about what happened when I was in eighth grade, while sitting in our living room, while I listened, dying, from my bedroom.

If I were her sponsor, I would've counseled her to leave that crap alone. She didn't. She confessed it all.

Boom. The sound of an explosion.

Nobody knew Grace had anything to do with my bad behavior back in the day.

Boom. The sound of an explosion.

Mom snarled at Grandma Gin for harboring a "whore" and a "junkie."

Another explosion.

Grandma Gin loved Grace as much as me by then. No way in hell would she fire her.

Another explosion.

Mom made me quit working at Dairy Queen, even though I had been earning money there since I was a little kid. "You will not step foot in that establishment, Isaiah," she told me.

Another explosion.

Mom made me go to Grace's house, knock on the door, ask Grace out on the stoop, and tell Grace, while Mom watched, that I would never speak to her again and that she would have to stay away from me or Mom would come after her legally.

Grace cried. Grace said sorry to me over and over. Mom shouted to me from the car to hurry up.

I chose Mom over Grace.

No more explosions.

Dad had moved out. Hannah was dead. Grandpa John was dead. I couldn't lose Mom. I stayed away from Grace. I went back to weight lifting, running, hitting people as hard as a speeding pickup truck when I was on the football field. But I didn't go easily. I promised myself I wouldn't be with any other girl. Grace or nobody. Grace or loneliness.

Go to bed early, get up early, work out, review homework, shower, get a ride from Riley's dad for weight lifting, go to school, work out/practice, homework/work, go to bed early.

But then my cracked bell. And Grace was in Grandma's backyard. I saw her there. I couldn't unsee her.

And my chest ached for Grace. I just wanted to see her again. We didn't have to talk. I knew she was at Dairy Queen. I looked at Grandma's work calendar on the wall all the time. I saw who was working and when. I knew Grace was there Monday through Thursday from 3 p.m. to close, Saturday from noon to close.

I parked Mom's Subaru in a neighborhood two blocks away and I walked. When I got close, instead of heading in from the front, I climbed up the hill behind the store. There I sat, next to some bushes, partially hidden.

From that vantage, I could see her. Grace worked the drive-through window. It was a warm day for early October. Lots of moms were bringing kids in after school. Busy. Grace leaned out the window. She turned the Blizzard over (a Dairy Queen stunt) to show how thick the ice cream treat was before handing the cup to the mom or kid. I could see her hands. I could see her wrists. I loved her bony wrists.

I wanted to talk to her, too, but wouldn't. I couldn't.

I watched the window for probably a half hour. Waited, holding my breath for her to bring the next ice cream out so I could see her again. Waited, still as I could be. Breathed when I could see her. Then it occurred to me that I was acting stupid. Is that what I'd become? Is that what my energy would transform into? Some kind of creeper hiding in a goddamn bush? A bolt of adrenaline shot through my limbs.

I stood up, shocked at my own behavior. At the same moment, Grace leaned out the drive-through with a Blizzard. She turned it over and saw me simultaneously. She dropped the Blizzard between the window and the car. A small child in the car screamed. Our eyes locked, mine and Grace's. I froze for a second, then took off at a dead sprint.

Three minutes later, I lay on the grass in the yard adjacent to where I'd parked Mom's Subaru. I'd sprinted the whole way from Dairy Queen. The dizziness was as heavy as anything I felt the Saturday morning right after my bell cracked. It was tornadic. Don't even know how long I stayed on the ground. Got up when a dude walking his dog asked if I needed help.

I told him I didn't. That was a lie, too.

CHAPTER 17

OCTOBER 4: THURSDAY

I went to bed after dinner Wednesday night, right after the conversation I'd had with mom where I told her I'd spoken to Coach Reynolds and he understood our decision. "They'll figure out a way to deal with it," I lied.

"You're such a brave kid."

"Don't tell any of your clients. I don't want this getting around. Coach Reynolds hasn't announced anything to the team yet."

"The only person I've mentioned this to is Sarah," Mom said.

"You what?" I shouted.

Mom sat stunned. "I talked to Sarah. Of course. We're in the office all day together."

Sarah Davies, Mom's administrative assistant, who is married to Bob Davies, a State Farm insurance agent, who is the brother of Carl Davies, a middle school social science teacher and basketball coach, who plays golf all the time with Dave Dieter, the goddamn defensive coordinator of the football team. Sarah has asked Mom why I'm not accepting scholarship calls. Dieter told Carl Davies about the colleges requesting info on me and Carl Davies told Bob and Bob told Sarah and Sarah spoke to Mom and Mom said, "We decided long ago that Isaiah is staying in town for college." If the information flows that way, it's going to flow the other.

"I would appreciate you keeping your mouth shut," I said. "I have a life."

"Don't speak to me like that, Isaiah."

"I have a life," I repeated.

"I know that," she said.

But she didn't know anything.

A ticking time bomb. It would go off. In a small town there's little distance between a random lawyer and the head coach of the football team.

I didn't do any homework. I was broken, exhausted.

Exhausted? From what? Usually I burn 1,500 calories working out. I run every day. I lift every day (legs one day, upper body the next). And during football season, I practice on top of all that working out.

This exhaustion was different. I felt my soul start to leave my body again.

I got up later than usual Thursday morning. Riley showed up at the house to pick me up for weight lifting. I was in the bathroom when the doorbell rang (he'd texted, but my phone was still in the bedroom). Mom answered the door. I ran back into my room, tried to listen while I pulled on my shirt. I could hear Riley talking. I panicked. What if they talked about me?

"Well, I wouldn't call it sick, exactly," Mom said as I ran into the living room.

"What do you mean? Isaiah's not sick?" Riley asked.

"Not super sick. Not too bad. Feeling pretty good," I said.

"You okay?" Mom asked. "Not dizzy."

"Fine," I said, and headed out toward Riley's car.

"You didn't bring your gym bag. You not lifting today?" Riley asked while driving. "What the hell? You have to maintain, man. You want to be weak for the Prairie game?"

"Oh. No. I don't know. Need to get my physics assignment done. No time to work out."

"Me and Twiggs did it last night. Did you get our texts?"

"Phone died."

"Well, that sucks. We probably screwed it up. We weren't sure about the scientific notation Urness made us do, but you didn't . . ."

"I don't remember what Urness said. Is it different than regular scientific notation?"

"How the hell should I know?" Riley asked.

"Was I in class when he talked about it?"

"Yeah, dude. You were," Riley said. "Yesterday?"

"Oh yeah," I said. I felt panic rise again.

While Riley worked out, I went to the IMC and read the chapter for physics and did the assignment. It was easy enough.

Physics went okay, except Riley acted like I wasn't in the room. He wouldn't look at me. What did I do to deserve that? I wondered.

Then, in study hall while I was trying to get ready for my AP Lit course (again, I didn't do the assignment and couldn't remember what Ms. Bowen had talked about in class the day before), Coach Reynolds showed up and asked me to come into the hall with him. The panic exploded. Sarah Davies, Bob Davies, Carl Davies, Dave Dieter, Coach Reynolds. *You're quitting football? You're done with football? Your life is gone?*

I couldn't be done. I wouldn't be done. This wouldn't work. But I couldn't run away from him in the hallway. I'd tell him something. I'd tell him it was a mistake. I followed him out of the IMC.

Out there, he leaned against a bank of sky-blue freshman lockers.

"So?" he said.

"Hey?" I asked. "Yeah?"

"Any news?"

"About? What news?" I asked.

"News, Isaiah. Did you learn anything from the doctor last night?"

"Oh," I said. "No. Not really. I couldn't get in to see a doctor." My stomach was dropping hard. My heart pounded.

"What do you mean you couldn't get in?"

"There was a long line at urgent care and I . . . I just didn't feel good, so I went home."

"You went straight home?"

"Yes?" I said.

"Really?" he asked.

"I think?" I said.

"Do you know something funny?" Coach Reynolds asked.

"Not really," I said.

"My daughter was doing her piano lesson over on Ellen Street after school. You know Ellen Street?"

"I've heard of it, yeah," I said.

"Sure you have. Over by Dairy Queen, right?" he said.

"Yeah. That's right. Near Dairy Queen."

"My daughter—you've met Taylor, haven't you?"

"I have. Sweet kid," I said.

"Taylor said she saw you run right past Katie Lee's house. Katie Lee is Taylor's piano teacher. Her place is over there on Ellen Street. Taylor said you ran by there like the devil was chasing you."

"Huh. Weird," I said. By this point my stomach had dropped into my intestines and bounced back up into my throat. I could feel waves of heat rolling across my face, picking up balls of sweat. But I was also relieved. This wasn't about Sarah, Bob, Carl, Dieter, football. I focused hard, my brain whirred. I wasn't running from Satan. I was running from ghosts. *Focus!* I shouted to myself.

"So?" he asked.

"Fine," I said. I pretended anger. "Fine. Fine, okay?"

"Fine what, Isaiah?"

Good liars use the truth. I'm a good liar. *Use the truth to make space . . .* "I pretty much got knocked stupid at the end of the game last week. You remember that hit?"

"Yes," Coach Reynolds said. "I know what you're talking about. You dropped your head when you hit Dakota Clay. Worried me for a second."

"It was bad. I felt really sick driving home from the game, okay? I threw up later."

"Uh-oh."

"And I had to go to the emergency room Saturday morning because I was puking still. I'm sorry. I'm a little messed up. I've never missed a game, you know?"

"I know, bud."

"But here's the deal: the doctor won't let me play this week. I can't play. I mean, I've got an appointment Friday morning to check in . . . and I hope. I've been trying to get better without bringing my damn head injury to your attention, so maybe I could play on Friday. Guess that shit backfired."

As I talked, the tension slowly released from Coach Reynolds's face. He started nodding. He bit his upper lip with his lower teeth. When I finished speaking, he put his big paw on my shoulder. "Okay. Okay. Calm down, Isaiah. But you got to listen to me."

"What, Coach?" I said.

"If you *are* injured, you have to *tell* me. Your health is my first priority. I care about you, kid. And these head problems, man, it's nothing you want to mess with. No way. *So* don't worry at all. We got your back tomorrow. Skip practice tonight. Rest up.

Make sure you're rested for that doctor's appointment tomorrow. We don't want any false negatives. We want to get you cleared as soon as possible. In fact, as soon as you're out of that appointment, give me a call. I want an update. The big one is still a week out. Prairie game isn't for eight days. We're okay this week. We got your back, but we'll need you come next week."

"Okay. Okay. Sorry I haven't been straight with you about this, Coach. It just scared me. I don't want to miss a game."

"Understood. You had me very worried. But understood."

There was an awkward pause. Coach looked back and forth between my eyes, maybe trying to see the concussion inside me? Finally, I said, "I have to finish my English homework, so . . ."

Coach snapped out of it. "Right. Go get 'em, bud."

I walked back toward the study hall room.

"Hey, bud?" Coach called after me. "Can you tell me why you were you sprinting down Ellen Street yesterday?"

I stopped. My mind raced. It landed fast. "I was testing myself. Seeing if I could run hard and not feel dizzy."

"Oh," he said. "And the verdict?"

"I'm feeling better. I'm getting better."

"Good news. Good news. Go home after school. Rest up."

"Okay," I said.

I reentered the study hall room and exhaled hard. Then I couldn't concentrate at all. I went into my AP Lit course totally unprepared. I bombed a pop quiz on *The Bluest Eye*.

CHAPTER 18

ISAIAH THE MONK

On Wednesday evening, two days before I hit Dakota Clay with my head down, I met Joey Derossi after practice at a McMansion on Bluffton's north side, out by the golf course. It was supposed to rain the next day, and Joey had to finish cleaning gutters on the place before the owner got home from vacation. Joey had klieg lights aimed up at the roof. We worked into darkness on two ladders.

He was in a quiet mood, which meant he was talking quietly (not in the loud, boisterous way he normally went on), not that he was failing to talk.

"Sometimes, I don't think I live right, man," he said. "You know, I gather all this shit up in the barn to make stuff, make art or whatnot, but I don't ever make the art, I just keep finding scraps and trash to use when I finally decide to make the shit. But where's the damn art I'm not making?"

"In your mind?" I said.

"I do have the materials. I just don't know what to do with them because I really don't know what I'm about." The old barn on his family's property was really junked up, filled with weird objects Joey had collected through the years.

"You're about living a good life. About being a good person," I said.

"Maybe?" he said. He climbed down the ladder. Moved it six feet to the left, then climbed back up and started digging in the gutter again. "But I'm not moving forward. Feels like I should be moving forward. Like, I'm not that different from you, right? I'm my own kind of lonely, isolated monk boy. I spend most of my time in my own head. Like you, dude. You're a sports monk with pretend friends."

"I like Riley and Twiggs. That's not pretend. They're real friends."

"Whatever. They're not on your plane. But I'm not either. You know why? You know what you are, and you do specific stuff that proves it. I don't. I just talk about everything out there in the world. Talk, talk, talk. Meanwhile, you don't say shit half the time, but you get all these specific things done, all moving in one direction. I was thinking, maybe your monoculture is right? Maybe being focused on one thing—like you're doing with football—is good? Practicing deeply, not widely, even if you risk becoming a ghost town."

"I am worried about that, though. I don't want to be a ghost town."

"Of course it's scary, man. You're risking all your other possible futures, and for what? A violent, hyped-up kids' game."

"Ouch."

"Not ouch. Quality. You play a violent hyped-up kids' game with great quality. That's something."

"Okay?" I said.

"Don't you feel it? Don't you get something meaningful out of practicing deep, practicing that same football monk shit over and over?"

"I don't know. I love the game, but I don't know if being good at it is the biggest reason I do what I do."

"Why else would you practice so deep, if not for the sake of quality play?" Joey asked. He whipped a bunch of gunk down on our tarp below, then looked at me.

"I practice hard at this thing because I'm afraid of the opposite of practice."

"What do you mean the opposite?" he said. "What's the opposite?"

"I prefer working out to not working out," I said.

"What's not working out? Lying around?"

"No. I've never been able to sit still. It's more to be . . . idle with myself, alone with myself and my random thoughts. That's bad for me, for real."

"Maybe that's what I am? Idle with myself?"

"I can't be idle. It's not only football. I study hard for school.

Read stuff about the stuff we're studying in school, because I don't get enough context from classes."

"Right. That's practicing deep."

"Maybe? It's just not being idle with myself."

"What does idle mean to you, though?"

"I don't know. It's the trembling void."

"Dude. You are so bad with your verbalization. Like your mouth doesn't do shit, sometimes."

"I have to think. Should I write?"

"Fine. Write. Let's get this damn gutter done. I need to be with my drums."

Joey had bought a three-piece cocktail drum set after he saw a jazz combo play on a street corner in Madison. He hoped to learn to play, even though he wasn't taking lessons. The truth is, he didn't need drums. He has plenty of things to do. He just never gets good at any one thing, I guess? Anyway, that night, I wrote this for him in my green notebook.

The Opposite of Practicing?

Before, he was antsy. He was anxious. He couldn't sit still. He was itchy on his insides. Before his sister died, he felt like a cartoon character stuck in a human world. In first grade, in the middle of quiet work time, he had an itchy voice in his head that told him to stand on his chair. He told the voice no. He told the voice he didn't want to stand on his chair. He told the voice he didn't want to get in trouble again. He begged the voice to leave him alone.

The voice said, "Do it now."

No, he said.

"Do it," the voice said.

No.

"Do it now!" the voice said again.

And so, he slowly stood up, slowly climbed onto his chair and spread his arms out like Jesus on the cross. Everyone, all the little kids, looked up at him with their eyes wide. Mrs. Johns, his teacher, shook her head back and forth fast. Her mouth opened.

He locked eyes with her. He mouthed, "Sorry."

"Get down off that chair, Isaiah Sadler."

He fell off the chair and broke his wrist.

This itchy voice didn't go away. It was part of him, too. Do it, the voice said. Everything is stupid. People are stupid. Show them you don't care, because you know how stupid this whole world is.

Do it.

And after his sister died, the voice lit a short fuse on a bomb. He and Reid broke all the windows at C & J Seed Company one night. By himself he took apart all the stalls in the eighth-grade bathroom. He took a knife and cut bike tires in the middle school bike rack. Nobody knew he had a hand in any of that.

Often, though, when the bomb went off, he was caught. He, Ben, and Reid set fire to five Christmas trees in Smith

Park. Ben and Reid ran away. He couldn't until it was too late.

And he didn't want the bomb to go off ever. He cried after the bomb went off. But his itchy voice remained. "Do it," the voice said. Everything is stupid, and you have to show them.

The life of the football monk didn't silence the itchy voice. Still, today, the voice sometimes tells him, "Do it." But, now, he doesn't do it. Before, if he tried to disobey the voice, he would find himself sitting by himself, bouncing up and down, thinking about "doing it," feeling so itchy, sweaty, desperate, afraid of himself, because he knew at any given moment his body might take off and he'd see with his eyes his own out-of-control hands hurling rocks at passing cars.

That is the opposite of practice to him.

After he became a football monk, when he disobeyed the voice he did so with a concrete activity. "Sorry, no time to throw rocks at cars, I have to lift weights so I'm ready for the next obstacle on the football field." Or, "Sorry, no time to do shots of schnapps. I have to complete a chemistry assignment before bed so I'm ready to meet Riley for gassers in the morning. He's depending on me...."

Being a football monk always provides an answer for the voice. He doesn't "do it" because he has work to do. And because he repeatedly does this important work, he finds himself being asked by people who have learned to *trust him to do more important work. Finishing important work, doing it well, never makes him cry (like breaking all the windows at C & J Seeds made him cry). He is no longer a destroyer. He is a builder. And the construction work he does always feels like a beginning, not an end. Each brick he adds to the building takes him higher. He will build the biggest tower in the world because he can always tell this voice that tells him to "do it," sorry, no, I've got so many other things I'd rather do than destroy.*

He doesn't know why building a tower feels better. He doesn't know its purpose. Practice doesn't tell him where he's going but tells him he's going somewhere good.

After Joey read it, he stared at me for a second, then grabbed the top of his head with both hands. "Your brain, man! You have competing brain modules working against each other. I totally get it."

"Yeah. Definitely. Like a good angel and a bad one inside me."

"Your ancient lizard brain shouts and your evolved human brain says *no thanks, lizard dude.* I have the same thing to some extent. I mean, I have conversations with myself a lot. My calm self is always telling my wacked lizard self to calm the hell down."

"Yeah," I said. "That."

"I always figured you were running away from something and you were running scared."

"I'm running away from the lizard void."

"But there's the other half. There's something even more important."

"There is?"

"You don't know where the running will go, but you know it's leading someplace better, so you keep running."

I thought for a second. I thought about the dreams I was having with Hannah, trying to stop her from getting in the car with Ray Gatos. "What if all the running actually doesn't lead someplace better, though? What if I get tired of running? What if the lizard void catches up to me? Like, the pickup truck is coming, you know? It's going to hit the car at some point."

"No. Just keep running, bro. Keep up the practice. Keep on trucking. Keep the faith and never do the opposite," Joey said. "You're building a big, beautiful tower!"

"We're working a lot of metaphors here," I said.

"We're making life mean something, man!" Joey said.

CHAPTER 19

OCTOBER 4: THURSDAY NIGHT

I went home after school and took a nap for three hours. In doing so, I missed the traditional night-before-the-game dinner at Steve's Pizza.

For the last couple of falls, every Thursday, day before game day, after the team walk-through out on the practice field, Twiggs, Riley, and I went to Steve's Pizza. Every Thursday we each ate an entire large pizza.

It probably wasn't good for us, physically. But it was good for our spirits. We'd talk about football and school and sometimes Twiggs and Riley would talk about girls (and I'd listen and smile, but say nothing about Grace). It worked for us. Since moving to varsity sophomore year, we'd only lost six games. Five were when we were sophomores, and just one, the state semifinals, last year.

Eating pizza at Steve's the day before a game was part of our victorious tradition. I broke it.

Where the hell are you? Riley texted.

Why didn't you tell us you had a concussion, dude? Twiggs asked.

Sorry. I don't know. I'm resting up. I'm a little messed up.

Neither Riley nor Twiggs replied.

I lost my breath. I stared at the walls of my bedroom. It was getting dark, sun going down.

My phone buzzed. I looked at the screen, hoped it was my friends. But it wasn't. Coach Conti from Cornell wrote:

How about tonight? Are your parents home? Let's get you set up for your visit!

Then, all at once, two other texts blew in. The first was from a number I didn't recognize.

I saw you watching me. Why? Don't answer. Ask yourself.

I knew who it was from. Her identity was confirmed a second later.

I got this message from my dad:

Are you available tonight? Grace Carey is concerned
about your behavior. Could you come over, please?

Grace Carey? What the hell did Dad have to do with Grace?
She was at Grandma's house two days ago and now Dad was
texting me on her behalf? What the hell was that about?

Yeah. Okay. I'll be over.

Mom stays at work late on Thursdays to meet with clients who can't meet during business hours. So I didn't have to
explain why I was going to Dad's place or, conversely, to lie to
her about going.

Unfortunately, Mom had taken her car. I went into the garage
and climbed on my old, barely used eighth-grade bike and
made my way across town. The rusty heap creaked underneath
me. Dad lives in an efficiency apartment above his engineering department colleague's garage. The place is a couple miles
away, across the street from campus.

I could've thought of many things while biking. Riley and
Twiggs. Coach Conti and Cornell. Mom, Coach Reynolds, or
the physics test I was supposed to take the next day. But I didn't
think of any of that. Instead, I felt good, pumping the creaking
pedals, the wind blowing around me, picking up speed. Move-
ment makes me calm.

I hid my bike under the rickety staircase that leads to Dad's place. I climbed the stairs, entered without knocking. Dad sat on the couch, watching MSNBC, eating Kraft Macaroni and Cheese (he has the taste buds of a fourth grader). There were engineering texts and student assignments on graph paper covering the coffee table in front of him.

He looked up. "The Republicans are no longer Republicans," he said. "They've turned into goddamn fascists. All they care about is keeping the rich, rich."

"Same old same old," I said.

"The hell it is," he shouted. "Everybody has to get their damn heads out of their damn asses, do you understand? Look at this!" He turned up the volume and the people on a panel spoke animatedly about whatever it was that had jacked Dad up.

I watched but didn't listen. This is one of the ways my family had gone crazy. Politics. What's stupid is they're all Democrats but still hate each other. Mom hates Bernie Sanders as much as she hates Trump. Dad thinks the Clintons destroyed the party. Grandma loves Joe Biden but thinks all the other national politicians are bad for American business, which makes both Mom and Dad call her a fascist. This is another reason they have a hard time sitting in a room together.

I miss Grandpa John. He wouldn't have put up with the family coming apart because of politics. He believed everybody has a "glass ass," which meant a weak spot. Instead of kicking at a person's glass ass, he said, we should remember that we've got one, too, and that someone might come along and kick ours if we're not smart enough to know we're not perfect ourselves.

"Hand out cushions for their glass asses. That's one way to

be a good friend," he told me after he calmed a fight between Mom and Melinda one Thanksgiving."

Grandpa John was military and a cop and about as tough as a dude could be, but he was nice to the bone, too. He literally tried to do good.

Speaking of good. Maybe Dad was trying to do good.

I sat down on a beat-up office chair next to the coffee table. "You wanted to see me?" I said over the noise.

Dad looked up, stunned out of his TV trance. He reached for the remote and turned the volume down. "Yes I did. Why in the hell would you hide behind Dairy Queen and jump out at Grace Carey?" he asked. "What were you doing away from school? Why weren't you at practice? What is going on?"

"I have a concussion. I can't practice," I said.

"You're still on the team. You don't leave the team just because you're injured. Or are you quitting because things are tough for you for the first time?"

"Are you talking about tough in football or tough in life, generally?" I asked.

"Football!" he shouted.

He had quit my family, left me behind, started a new life, moved into a tiny apartment that made it impossible for me to stay overnight. I glared at him. He'd made my life tough.

"So? What do you have to say, Isaiah?"

I sniffed. Focused. "Coach Reynolds asked me to pick up his daughter from piano lessons, since I couldn't practice with the team. I was early, so I went on a walk to kill time. I didn't mean to scare Grace. I didn't even know she was working."

"Really?" Dad asked.

"Yeah," I said. "It was just a weird situation."

"Well, good. But . . . listen. So you know . . . there are just some things you should know about Grace," he said.

"Why? I barely think about her now."

"Good. She doesn't want you to think about her."

My stomach tightened. "That's fine," I said. "I don't. Ever."

"Then what in the hell made you hide behind a bush next to Dairy Queen?" he asked.

"I already explained that. What's the deal with Grace? Why is it such a big deal?"

"Grace thinks of you as her role model," Dad said.

My mouth opened, but no words fell out.

"The way you've turned your life around, Isaiah. What you've been able to do."

"Oh," I said. "That's nice."

"It is. But I'm worried for her. I don't have to tell you, Grace doesn't come to the table with the same good cards you were dealt."

"What good cards are those?"

"Don't be obtuse, Isaiah," Dad said. "You might have been beat up when you came to the table to play, but you had a great set of cards."

"My dead sister card? My murdered grandpa card? My parents who hated me? Are those the cards you're referring to?"

Dad took in my words for a moment. His face reddened. "Parents who hated you?"

"You sent me away."

"You needed help. We couldn't provide the help you needed," Dad said.

"Mom brought me home before I completed the treatment program."

"She missed you, Isaiah."

"Isn't that selfish?"

Dad breathed for a moment. "Listen to me. Your mother had lost her daughter. She was wrecked. She's still wrecked if you haven't noticed."

Is that why you left? I thought. *Your wife was too damaged for you to deal with anymore?* "I know," I said. "I feel sorry for Mom."

"I do, too," Dad said. "But Grace's situation is different than yours. There are bad things happening in that house. Ongoing, you know? An ongoing tragedy."

I nodded. "Grace's mom is a train wreck."

"Nothing like that piece-of-trash stepfather of hers."

"He's bad. I know."

"You can't possibly understand how bad, Isaiah," Dad said.

"Uh" is all I could muster.

"His presence in the house made it impossible for Grace to graduate from high school, right? It makes it impossible for her to be safe. That's not her fault."

"Yeah," I said. How did he know this stuff?

Dad nodded, showing he knew more. "Grace has been on her own since she was sixteen. Do you know she bought her

115

own groceries with her Dairy Queen money because these supposed adults in her house wouldn't feed her?"

"I know," I said. "We were friends then."

"Lucky for Grace . . . somehow your fascist grandmother has seen fit to pay her well and to give her more and more responsibility and pay her better. That church you've started going to has given her an AA group to attend."

"Grandma's church. I just drive Grandma. It's not my church." This was sort of a lie. "Don't worry."

Dad looked confused. "Why would I worry?"

"Because you're Jewish."

"I'm as Jewish as your mother is Christian. I don't give a shit what you do if it gives you some joy or sustenance. Don't you know that?"

"I know," I said, although this was news to me.

"Isaiah, Grace earned her GED last spring. Your grandmother asked me to step in and help get her ready for college. I got Grace into an ACT prep course over the summer." Dad began to tear up. He had a hard time speaking. "She got her scores on Monday. She did well."

"On the ACT?"

"Twenty-five," Dad said. "A twenty-five from nothing."

"That's because . . . you and Grandma have been helping Grace. You didn't tell me anything about it."

"Why would I? You don't think about Grace," Dad said.

"But I care about her. Probably more than you do."

"Not more than Gin. Did you know your grandmother

provides health insurance to her full-time employees? And that she only has one full-time employee? She pays for Grace's health insurance. That insurance has allowed Grace to go into therapy."

"Grandma says therapy is bullshit," I said. "She told Mom it's bullshit."

"Apparently Gin has different rules for different people. She's encouraged Grace to go to therapy. Grace has been working hard on it. And . . . and I shouldn't tell you this—Grace took me into her confidence—but I want to protect her . . . and you, so I'm going to say this. You don't think about Grace, but she thinks about you. You're in her thoughts constantly. Some tripped-up part of her believes you're her destiny. That you make everything better. She thinks you saved her from suicide back when she was . . ."

I stood up. "I need to see her right now," I said.

Dad stood up. "What?"

"I want to see her."

"No. Are you listening, Isaiah?"

"She needs me," I said.

"Exactly wrong. She needs to leave you behind like you left her behind. I'm telling you to stay away from her, on the off chance that you weren't, in fact, helping your coach yesterday, but were, in fact, hiding behind Dairy Queen so you could force an encounter with Grace."

"I wasn't trying to force anything."

"Good, because Grace doesn't need . . . She cannot have

you barreling in there and messing her up, Isaiah. She's close to pulling herself out. There's no future between the two of you."

"Why not?" I asked.

"You said you don't think about her."

"Why shouldn't we have a future?"

Dad shook his head, like he was trying to shake out cobwebs. "Because you're you. You're not going to be here after this year, Isaiah. You'll go to college and then start your adult life someplace else. It won't be here. What's here for you? But for Grace? What else does she have? She may well end up owning the Dairy Queen."

"Wait. Our Dairy Queen?"

"Your grandmother's Dairy Queen."

"Our family's Dairy Queen."

"You haven't set foot in Dairy Queen for years."

"It's more my Dairy Queen than Grace's," I spat.

Dad sort of laughed. It was an odd reaction. "Isaiah? What is wrong with you?" he asked.

"Mom wants me to stay here for college."

"So? Your mother doesn't choose your college."

"I'm staying here. I won't leave here. I deserve some happiness."

"Bullshit," Dad said. "Why would you stay here? You could go to Madison to study or play football at a great Division III school somewhere. You can't stay here. That's ridiculous."

"I committed to Bluffton."

"Not true. I've told Coach Reed a thousand times not to

118

count on you staying in town."

"Have you talked to Mom ever?" I said.

"She's saying you have to stay here?" Dad asked. "What in the hell is going on in that house of yours? Why aren't we talking about this? Have you looked at other colleges, Isaiah? Haven't you been recruited?"

"Yes."

"Well?" Dad asked.

"I told them I'm staying here."

"Why? What's your ACT? You haven't even told me your ACT. Is it okay? You could go to New York City or Houston or Boston, Isaiah. Seattle! Portland! I know you get good grades."

"Do you?" I said.

"Of course I do. So?"

"So what?" I said.

"Isaiah, come on," Dad said. "You own your future. No one else does."

I took in a deep breath. This is the thought that bloomed in my cracked bell: Grace and I could own Dairy Queen together. Good life. Perfect. Meaningful. My next life. "I have to go," I said.

"No," Dad said.

"Yes," I said.

"Do not go and see Grace. Please," Dad said.

"I just want to go think." I felt dizzy. I don't think it had to do with the concussion. But I am injured. My bell began cracking a long time ago. Before the hit in the Lancaster game. The dizziness didn't have to come from an injury on the field to be a symptom of a grave injury. My bell is broken.

I scrambled to the door. Dad followed behind me, talking the whole way.

"You won't go see Grace? We can talk more about this. I'm sorry I didn't tell you I've been helping her. I've always felt for the girl. I've always thought she was more positive than negative in your life. Just let her . . . let her breathe, okay?"

"I just want to think," I repeated.

I opened the door.

Dad called out behind me, "Will you please tell me your goddamn ACT score?"

And, for some reason, I didn't lie. "Thirty-two," I shouted over my shoulder.

"Oh Jesus Christ, Isaiah!" he yelled.

ACT? Who cares?

No more football?

Then Grace. Because why not? Everything is stupid. The world is stupid. There is no point to this endless suffering and bullshit.

I biked around town for two hours without doing it, without going to see Grace, but the voice in my head said, do it. I tried to think about other things, get my mind to relax, but there was no good place for my mind to go.

When I got home, instead of going inside, I sat down on the cold back stoop and googled how many kids die in car accidents each year. Answer? A lot. So damn many. Thousands.

CHAPTER 20

OCTOBER 4: THURSDAY NIGHT

I couldn't sleep. I opened my green notebook and read what I wrote for Joey Derossi the morning after the Glendale game.

This Is Why

The moon is a great, bright eyeball staring down from blackest space. Below, stadium lights make the colors vibrate. Yellow uprights. Green field. White away jerseys. Cardinal-and-gray home. The marching band warms up, one minute to halftime. The guys on the tenor drum sets pound a rhythm that bursts inside Isaiah's chest. Boom. Tick, tick, tick, tick, tick, tick. Bada boom boom. Tick, tick, tick, tick . . .

This is it. Where he has belonged. Out on that green field with the eyeball looming, with the percussion exploding his chest.

He can't help it. He looks up. He says, "Thank you."

And then Isaiah locks in.

The quarterback shouts numbers. Isaiah checks out the action in the backfield. His opponent is faking a run play. Seriously. Pretending. "Be ready for pass. Be ready!" Isaiah cries.

Simultaneously, the opponent quarterback yells, "Hut!"

No run. Isaiah nailed his call. The quarterback drops.

"Pass! Pass!" Isaiah shouts.

The slot receiver goes off the line slow, like he's not even in the play. But suddenly, like the kid is hit with a bolt of electricity, he explodes forward. Tries to break out of the jail Isaiah built for him. And the kid does get behind Isaiah.

So Isaiah swivels, sprints after.

The quarterback jacks the ball high into the air. Isaiah sprints. The ball must be reaching apex. Isaiah sprints. Must be falling, spiraling, nose down toward the slot receiver's outstretched hands. Isaiah sprints.

Then he digs in deep.

Leaps.

And he grabs that damn ball a millisecond before the slot receiver can.

Gathers, tucks, rolls on the turf.

Comes to a stop. Breathes. There is silence. His sinuses drain.

The sound of the ocean comes. The sound of the wind ripping through ditches on the razor-backed ridges.

He leaps up, ball over his head.

"Bluffton interception," the away-game announcer says.

"Thanks for running that route," Isaiah says to the slot in all seriousness. "That was a close call. Nice try."

"Shut up, dude," the slot says, walking away.

The drums reverberate in Isaiah's chest. He runs to his screaming team on the sidelines and leaps into their arms.

CHAPTER 21

OCTOBER 5: FRIDAY MORNING DOCTOR'S APPOINTMENT

The appointment was at 11 a.m. Mom gave me the choice, and I chose not to go to school before. I stayed in bed for as long as I could.

In bed, I made a plan. I'd tell the doctor I hadn't had a symptom since Monday. I'd tell him I sprinted (by accident) and rode my bike for ten miles the night before. I'd tell him I felt great, good to go, ready to get back to playing my game. I repeated this over and over in my head. I wouldn't just sit there and let Mom do the talking about the decision *we'd* made. I'd made no decision at all.

Dad was already in the parking lot when we arrived at the doctor. He diverted all attention.

"Did you make Isaiah commit to Bluffton for college?" he

barked the moment Mom shut the car door behind her.

"I didn't make him do anything. We had a conversation. We came to the same conclusion. He won't have to pay tuition because you're a professor here. He won't run up loans. He'll get a wonderful education. He'll put himself ahead of the game."

"Thirty two on his ACT," Dad said. "Nobody told me thirty-two! Do you even register the opportunities you're taking away from him?"

Mom glared. Mom inhaled. "We have a doctor's appointment. Now is not the time."

"If I hadn't asked Isaiah over last night I might never have known about his ACT. Clearly you weren't going to tell me!" Dad shouted.

Mom swung her intense gaze to me. "You went to your dad's last night? Why is that? Didn't you go out for pizza with your friends?"

"I'm going inside." I turned and walked in. My parents didn't immediately follow. Both were red-faced when they finally got to the waiting room. They sparred. I pulled out earbuds and listened to nothing. I just wanted them to know I didn't care about their conversation.

The trouble continued after we got in front of the doctor.

He looked into my eyes. Had me do a balance test. Asked me a bunch of questions about my memory, my sensitivity to light and sound, and my dizziness. I told him I felt normal, which was true, physically speaking.

"I rode my bike last night. A couple of days ago, I took off running before I remembered I was supposed to avoid doing that kind of thing. I feel totally fine," I said.

He took a couple of notes on his clipboard. "You look good, Isaiah. If you're feeling normal and have already engaged in exercise, there's no reason not to return to your normal activities."

"What?" Mom asked. "Return? Do you mean return to football?"

"He's not suffering from symptoms. There's no reason for him to hold back, unless symptoms crop up again," the doctor said. "If you have any dizziness or sudden loss of energy, you need to pull yourself out, do you understand?"

I didn't respond.

"Good. Good to hear," Dad said.

Mom pointed her pen at the doctor. "You told us last week that Isaiah shouldn't play football anymore."

"I said no such thing," the doctor said.

Mom turned the page back in her notebook, which she'd taken out to take notes. "Six days ago you warned us about second impact syndrome. You said he shouldn't play."

"No, I said if Isaiah were my child I'd pull him. I'm not his parent. I'm treating him. Isaiah has cleared protocol. As his doctor, I'm telling you he's clear to go back to his regular activities."

"I'm ready," I said.

Mom stood up from her chair. "Oh, no you don't. I'm your

parent. There will be no second impact syndrome. You've already notified the team."

"Have I?" I said.

"You better have," Mom said.

"I'm his parent, too," Dad said. He stayed seated in his chair. "You seem to have forgotten this inconvenient truth, Tammy."

Mom swiveled on him. "Oh, you're interested now?" she said. "Now that you have an opportunity to put Isaiah in harm's way, you're ready to jump in, give him permission?"

"Isaiah does not belong to you," Dad said. "It's time for you to step back and let him make choices about his future. He got a thirty-two on his ACT, for God's sake!" Dad shouted.

For a moment there was silence.

"Wow. That's a good score," the doctor said. "Are you looking at any tier-one schools?"

"Tier one?" I asked.

"Ivies," Dad said. "Or heavy-hitting liberal arts colleges."

Mom slowly sank back into her chair.

There was another moment of silence.

Then I said, "I've been talking to a coach at Cornell University."

"You have?" Dad asked, surprised.

"Yes. I have," I said.

Mom sat forward. "What are you talking about, Isaiah? When?"

I pulled out my phone and showed them the last text from Coach Conti.

How about tonight? Are your parents home? Let's get you set up for your visit!

"That's really from Cornell?" Mom asked.

I nodded.

"Great school!" the doctor said.

"Stay out of this," Dad said to him.

CHAPTER 22

OCTOBER 5: PIECE OF SHIT

One of the reasons Joey Derossi suggested I write my life in third person was so I could be objective, right? So I could treat myself as a character, to separate from the emotion.

Green notebook time.

PIECE OF SHIT

They went to Steve's Pizza after the doctor's office because they didn't know what else to do.

Cornell.

"It's not a big deal," Isaiah said. "They didn't offer me a scholarship. There's not a letter of intent ready for me. I don't even know how that would work, since they don't give actual athletic scholarships."

"I can't afford to send you to Cornell," Mom said.

"If they want Isaiah to play, you won't pay a cent for that education, Tammy," Dad said. "You think Cornell University doesn't have money to bring in the athletes they want? They may not give traditional athletic scholarships in the Ivies, but they sure as hell pay athletes to show up."

"Yeah," I said. "Coach Conti said they make offers. Full offers. It's need-based, most of the time. He said they'd put together a package because they know I'm not rich."

Mom and Dad both stared at me for a moment. I'd betrayed more information than I wanted to.

"How do they know you're not rich?" Dad asked. "Did you send them a piece of torn notebook paper written on with a crayon from the hippie who pays you cash for painting houses?" Dad choked on his soda, laughing.

No one else laughed.

"Isaiah? How does Cornell know anything about you?" Mom asked.

"Conti is their defensive backs coach. He saw me play at Glendale in August and it's not like my life is a secret. There's video of me playing online . . . and I sent him some, too."

"Glendale? You've been talking to Cornell since August and you haven't told us?" Dad asked. He turned to Mom. "Why the hell do you think that is, Tammy? Why would he hide wonderful news?"

"No. That's not what I mean. How do they know you aren't rich?" Mom whispered.

Isaiah took stock of her face. "Maybe you already know?" he said.

Mom nodded slowly, the truth dawning. "I thought my files looked strange a few weeks ago. My financial folder wasn't flush with the others."

"Oh my God. Really?" Dad said. "You think Isaiah stole your tax information?"

"I did," Isaiah said. "I scanned your taxes for the last three years. That's what Cornell asked for, so that's what I gave them."

"Wow," Dad said. "Resourceful."

Mom shook her head minutely, her eyes watering. He hadn't seen her look this way in a few years. Fury was building.

"So? What?" Isaiah asked.

"You tricked me again, didn't you?"

"Again?" Isaiah said.

"You've just gotten so good at this thing you do, I stopped seeing what you are."

He could've apologized at that moment. He could've stopped the train from derailing, but he didn't. "What am I?" Isaiah asked quietly.

"What is he?" Dad asked. "What are you saying?"

"He's a liar," Mom said. "A cheat. It comes so naturally to him."

"That's not fair," Dad said. "He's looking after his own future. And for God's sake, that's exactly what he should be doing."

"By stealing my personal information," Mom said. "Cornell University has my social security number? They know how much I make? What else, Isaiah?"

"Nothing," Isaiah said. "Bank statements. 401(k). Et cetera."

Mom was trembling. Tears were getting thick in her eyes. "Oh, brilliant. Makes no difference to you, though, does it? Go ahead and lie, pretend you're a good kid, make me believe in you."

"Tammy. Come on, calm down," Dad said.

"But you're not a good kid, are you? You're the same lying piece of shit you always were," she said to Isaiah. "You learned to play me, but you're just the same."

Since sophomore year, when Dad unceremoniously left the house, Isaiah and his mom had become a unit. Yes, Isaiah told her what she wanted to hear. No, he didn't express his darker thoughts to her. But still, they grew close. Legitimately close. They had a movie night every week. They went to England together for ten days a summer ago. They spent a week one Christmas at a golf resort in Scottsdale, Arizona (strange, as neither played golf). The rift from before healed. Isaiah knew his mother manipulated him. And he wasn't honest with her all the time. But he forgave her for losing her mind when Hannah died. He forgave her for treating him badly when he was a messed-up fourteen-year-old who needed love more than anything. He knew she was hurt like he was hurt. She had caused *him pain, but he loved her, and he felt empathy for her. He forgave her.*

The same lying piece of shit?

Just like that, the empathy was gone.

Isaiah stood up and walked away.

"Isaiah!" Dad shouted.

Isaiah left the restaurant.

CHAPTER 23

OCTOBER 5: GAME DAY

I jogged all the way to school from Steve's Pizza. I didn't have my backpack. I didn't know where else to go. I had to go back to school. I cried a little on the way, turning sideways to hide my face from cars that passed by. I needed to go suit up, play the game. That's what my plan was. I'd play football with my team.

The first person I saw in the commons was Mr. Urness, my physics teacher. He was on his way out as I entered. He carried a giant pile of papers in a fabric grocery sack. "Mr. Sadler," he said. He showed me the papers. "You were absent for the unit test. Still feeling sick?"

"I . . . yes. I was at the doctor this morning." I completely forgot the test.

"You look healthy now," he said.

"Clean bill of health, I guess," I said.

"Four hours too late," he said.

"Sorry. I know. I didn't want to go to the doctor . . . because I wanted to take the test."

"We'll discuss this next week. I'm headed to my niece's wedding in Iowa."

"Okay," I said.

"She's marrying a bozo," he said.

I moved past him, into the school. I couldn't remember where I was supposed to be. English? Maybe? Two freshmen girls worked on a volleyball banner on the commons floor. "What period is it?" I asked.

"Fifth?" one said, like it was a question.

"Don't you know?" I asked.

"You don't," she said.

"It's fifth period," the other said flatly.

But right as I got to English, the bell rang, and my classmates began flowing out from the room, pushing me backward.

It was Friday. I had Current Events, essentially a class where seniors watch CNN, and then I had a study hall last period. The day couldn't end fast enough. I texted Twiggs to see if he wanted to meet me in the locker room instead of going to study hall.

I saw that Mom had texted me fifteen times. She'd apologized again and again.

I felt nothing but rage.

Be there, Twiggs texted back.

CHAPTER 24

OCTOBER 5: GAME DAY II

"Don't you think it's pretty weird, dude, that we kept asking you if you were injured from that hit, but you lied and said you had the flu?" Twiggs asked. We sat on a bench outside the school, looking over the practice field. He wore his game jersey, like we all do on game days, except I didn't have mine on. I hadn't even thought about it that morning.

"Yeah," I said. "Yeah. I don't know why I lied. I didn't want anyone to know about my concussion. It sounds worse than it is. My concussion. Not the lying part. That's bad."

"Well," Twiggs said. "It'll be fun in some ways, you know? Pretty much Riley hasn't played defense since we were freshmen."

I'd played some offense that year—running back. Riley had

136

played my position, strong safety, and had been pretty good, although not as good as me because I like hitting and he doesn't. "Riley?" I said. "Strong safety?"

"He didn't tell you? Reynolds is going to start him both ways, QB and strong safety. If we get up quick—which we should, because who the hell is River Valley? They haven't won a damn game all year . . . Reynolds will let Willis take over."

Willis, a sophomore, was my backup, but he rarely got in. Never occurred to me that Riley would start at my position. *My position . . .*

My stomach balled up in a knot.

"Won't be necessary. Riley doesn't need to do that. I'm playing. Doctor said I could go back to normal activities. I'm in."

"Ha ha," Twiggs said.

"Ha ha?" I asked.

"Well. No, you aren't playing," he said. "You didn't practice all week. You had a concussion. We're playing River stupid Valley, who we can beat without you. You didn't even show up for pizza last night. You've been lying and acting like a dumbass, and that says to me and to everyone else, you aren't playing, dude. You're some kind of alien version of yourself right now. You'll probably drop your eyes again if you play right now. You want to get injured for life? Wait and play next week against Prairie, when we need you and when your scrambled brain isn't leaking out of your damn ear, okay?"

"No," I said. "I have to play."

"Dude, what the hell?" Twiggs said. "I'm super dumb, but

I'm not dumb enough to play the week after a concussion like you got. That's just ridiculous. Coach isn't going to let you play, anyway."

"Shit, shit, shit," I said. I dropped my head into my hands.

"You'll be okay, buddy." Twiggs patted me on the back. "Next week will be here soon."

CHAPTER 25

OCTOBER 6: THE GAME

I twisted in my sheets. I rolled and turned on the light next to my bed. I picked up my phone and saw that it was 2:21 a.m. *Shit,* I thought. My head vibrated, not from a concussion, but from unspent adrenaline. I grabbed my green notebook from the floor.

He Wasn't Allowed to Play

No, this wasn't because his mother had called the coach to tell him she wouldn't permit him to play. There had been no such communication. No, it wasn't because the doctor had told him that morning he could not play. What had the doctor said? The boy can return to his normal physical activities. It was punitive. He hadn't been at practice. He hadn't been engaged. Not even his teammates wanted him to play.

"Take a load off, bud. Hang close to Coach Dieter. Help make defensive adjustments if we need it," Coach Reynolds told him.

In every away game he'd played since freshman year, he and Riley had shared a seat on the bus, both to and from the game. On the way, they talked about what would happen in the game—the specific strengths and weaknesses of the offensive and defensive systems they'd be facing and, after they moved to varsity and watched video of their opponents, the specific strengths and weaknesses of the players they'd be facing. On the ride home, they'd debrief. If the ride was long enough, they'd often discuss every play that had taken place during the game, dissecting the larger action, their reactions, their roles in the play's result. Again, it was tradition. It was what they did. Riley and Isaiah had never been best friends in the way friends are depicted on TV. They didn't seek solace in each other's company. They didn't text each other (not like Isaiah and Twiggs did) to see what was happening. Isaiah had once asked Riley if they'd stay in contact after graduation. Riley said, "Well, yeah, if we play at the same college." But don't misunderstand. Isaiah and Riley were best friends. Football made them best friends.

On the way to River Valley High School, a forty-five-minute drive across farmed ridges and into deep, forested ravines, Isaiah sat by himself, in the back of the bus. His normal seat next to Riley had been taken by running back, Iggy Eze. Riley hadn't even looked at Isaiah when he boarded.

The game unfolded as everyone expected. The River Valley Blackhawks acted like they didn't want to be on the field with Bluffton. They ran a scared, old-fashioned Wing-T offense. Sweeps with pulling guards (guards who were both small and slow). Dives, bellies, a single tackle-trap led by a tackle who was no more than 5'10" but easily weighed 300 pounds—Riley slid past him like lightning, popped the running back so fast the ball shot straight up in the air and then Riley had caught it, turned into the amazing offensive player he is, juked three different guys before barreling into the end zone to make the score 27–0 in the first quarter.

They were right. They didn't need Isaiah.

I put down my pen, closed my notebook, turned out the light above my bed. It was 2:47 in the morning. All this adrenaline in my body. I texted Joey Derossi, but he didn't answer. I walked into the kitchen to get a glass of water.

While running the water to make it cold, I looked out the back window.

Someone stood in Grandma Gin's backyard, smoking a cigarette.

I went out the back door. "Grace?" I shouted.

She didn't answer. She reentered the house.

I thought about what Dad had said, about how I should leave her be.

But she wasn't letting me be. She was staring at my house, waiting for me to come to her.

Honest to God! What the hell was Grace doing at Grandma's house at three o'clock in the damn morning? I almost went over to find out, but I stopped myself in the middle of the yard. I couldn't wake Grandma Gin at 3 a.m.

CHAPTER 26

OCTOBER 6: THE MEANING OF 3 A.M.

I wrote this, then forgot about it.

He Was Retired. But He Was Still a Hero.

At 8:25 p.m. on September 27 five years ago, a fourteen-year-old girl got into the car of a white male, age twenty-nine, in the parking lot of a Jimmy John's in suburban Milwaukee. It was caught on security cameras. She'd gone to the restaurant pissed off because she had to babysit her little brother and didn't want to. The girl already had a history of drug use, of trouble with the law. But her mother didn't have anywhere else to turn. The girl had to babysit her little brother because her mother had to go to her shift at the hospital. Police found out later, the girl's anger at being forced to babysit prompted her to get into this car. A little revenge against her mother. The white male offered her a chance to smoke some weed. The white male took the girl away.

The white male's name was Jeremy Chambers. He had a tattooed M on his neck, apparently an homage to the Big M, a well-known landmark on a hill near Bluffton, Wisconsin. Very identifiable. The police knew what car he was driving at the time, too. A black 2008 Pontiac Grand Am with a cracked back-left panel. What they didn't know was this: What the hell was he doing on the other side of the state from where he normally operated, moving weed and meth and sometimes heroin across southwest Wisconsin, northeast Iowa, and southeastern Minnesota?

Even though he was in suburban Milwaukee and not in his normal zone of activity, detectives at the Wisconsin Bureau of Criminal Apprehension immediately recognized both him and the car when they looked at the video footage. They were already in the midst of a larger investigation into a web of meth and heroin distribution that connected Chicago, Milwaukee, Minneapolis, and Des Moines and parts in between. Jeremy Chambers was a big player in the parts in between. He was also a well-known asshole.

At 12:30 a.m. on September 28, Isaiah's grandpa John Bertram, less than a year retired from his long career with the Wisconsin BCA, received a phone call from his good friend Mike Meisel, a BCA detective. Meisel conferenced him in with the Bluffton chief of police and the Grant County sheriff. Jeremy Chambers had been spotted pumping gas into his Pontiac at a Bluffton Kwik Trip gas station. He had exited the scene before police arrived. No girl was seen in the car, however.

There was credible camera evidence that Chambers had headed east of town, likely to his girlfriend's trailer, near where the larger County Road G turned into the one-lane Jericho Road. Grandpa Bertram knew the area well, knew the little dirt drives that pierced fields of corn and followed the jagged creek line of Mounds Branch. In the early 2000s he'd busted an isolated but large-scale meth production house in the same vicinity. He'd done so after months of surveillance, oftentimes on foot.

They asked him to meet them off Jericho Road. To direct them into some of these drives and dirt roads that might help them surround Chambers's location without tipping him or his girlfriend off. There was possibly a fourteen-year-old's life at stake. Grandpa Bertram didn't think twice about going, even though Grandma Gin had said, "I got a bad feeling."

She was right to have that bad feeling.

Grandpa John rolled up slowly, his headlights off, stopped his GMC Yukon behind tall grasses and a stand of burr oak close enough to the trailer where Chambers was purported to be. He could see the black Pontiac parked in the light that the trailer shed. Grandpa John stayed there, watching, waiting for his friend Meisel, BCA staff, and the local police to join him. Unfortunately, the situation turned fast. Grandpa John saw a figure leave the trailer and enter the Pontiac. The Pontiac came to life. Reversed, turned, and began exiting the property via a nearby drive. Grandpa John pulled out his cell and called Meisel.

"We're five minutes from your location, John," he was told.

"Aw shit," Grandpa John said. "Just got here, but he's leaving."

"Don't do anything," Meisel said. "We're close."

Grandpa John hung up. The Pontiac rolled down the drive. What could he do? Let Chambers leave? What about the girl? Grandpa turned the ignition, pulled the Yukon forward, drove it across the drive's exit.

Jeremy Chambers's girlfriend—because she was the one driving, not Chambers—stopped the Pontiac. Grandpa John climbed from the Yukon's cab, stayed hidden on the driver side, shouted over the car, "You just stay where you are, now. There are cops crawling all around the premises and we need to talk to you."

What Grandpa John didn't know was that Jeremy Chambers had spotted him a moment earlier. He'd seen the Yukon pull up. Not good. Chambers needed to get out on the road to make it to Prairie du Chien before sunrise. Chambers figured he had to do something about whoever was in that truck. He told his girlfriend to pull the car up the drive to draw attention. He'd surprise whoever it was in that GMC Yukon, have a chat.

Later Chambers told a detective, "I crept around the side of the trees over there. Figured it was a couple of teens, making out or something. Wanted to scare them off, so I could roll. . . ."

Bullshit. The moment Chambers saw Grandpa John, he raised a Glock 9mm and fired twice. My grandpa . . . Isaiah's Grandpa fell to the ground, dead. He never saw what was coming. The best dude in the world was gone just like that.

But it wasn't for nothing. Jeremy Chambers's girlfriend lost her mind when shots were fired. Got out of the car and ran back in the trailer screaming. Jeremy chased her down instead of leaving in the Pontiac. That was all the time the cops needed. They arrived in mass a few moments later.

When they got there, Chambers exited the back of the house and ran into the cornfields but was caught in minutes. His girlfriend was taken into custody without incident.

They searched the house and the Pontiac. A terrified, tied-up fourteen-year-old girl was found in the trunk. Based on information gained from Chambers's girlfriend on the scene, the fourteen-year-old was about to be driven to a farm near Prairie du Chien, Wisconsin. The cops went to the farm instead. Wisconsin BCA broke up a Minnesota-based sex-trafficking ring using the information the girl-friend gave them.

Grandpa John died for that fourteen-year-old girl and maybe lots of others like her.

Grandpa John's BCA friend Mike Meisel left the crime scene. He rang Grandma Gin's doorbell at 3 a.m. He wanted Grandma Gin to see how her husband, John Bertram, died. Blocking a driveway. Protecting the life of a child. Meisel knew Gin well enough to know she'd want to see exactly what happened.

She went out there to Jericho Road. She saw Grandpa John's body lying by the Yukon.

"That's a dream I had a lot. Seeing him like that," she told Isaiah later. "I always figured it would come to that. Was surprised he got to retirement in one piece, but he couldn't really retire."

I couldn't go over to Grandma's house at 3 a.m. Knock on the door like some bearer of biblically bad news . . .

Grandma Gin knew that Grace was there, though, right?

Was Grace staying there overnight?

She had to be.

I wanted to know. I wanted to see Grace.

My thoughts turned and turned and turned on the same item. Grace.

The sun was up before I fell asleep.

CHAPTER 27

OCTOBER 6: SATURDAY, NOON

I woke up at a little past noon. My phone buzzed twice from a single text.

Guess we don't need you. I can play strong safety!

It was from Riley, who barely talked to me Thursday. Riley, who hadn't saved a seat for me on the bus Friday. Riley, who had played my position against River Valley the night before.

He was right, too. He played my position great. What did he want me to say, though? *You're so much better at football than me!*

Good. I'm not going to play anymore.

He wrote back right away.

> Don't be a dick. I was just joking. I don't want to play
> strong safety.

Bullshit. He wanted to humiliate me. I didn't respond. He
was the dick.

And I wouldn't play anymore. That's what I decided in the
fever of my insomnia. Crack my brain for a hyped-up kids'
game? Play a stupid game, play for teammates who didn't care
about me.

A game. A stupid game. Totally meaningless. Nothing
changes whether you win or lose.

Joey Derossi was right. Isaiah Sadler would be happier without all that shit. Isaiah Sadler was done with monoculture.

Of course, Mom was sitting in the living room when I went
out there. She was waiting for me. I'd dressed already. I planned
on getting on my bike and going to find Joey to tell him the
news: I was wrong. I was done with monoculture. He was right
last summer when he told me about ghost towns. I was living in
one. Mom smiled.

"Slept in?" she said. "That's not like you."

I wasn't sure what to say. Seeing her filled me with burning
hatred I couldn't let loose if I expected to get out of the house.
"Uh" is what I landed on.

"You don't respond to texts anymore?" she asked.

I'd spent years accommodating her mourning, trying to

make up for Hannah by being a good mama's boy. "No," I said. "No more responses to texts."

"Why should I pay for your phone, then?" she asked, her face going red.

I had my phone in my hand. I reached out with it. "Then take it. I don't need your phone."

She stared at me for a moment without moving. She scanned my eyes. "Why are you so angry at me? Is this about football?"

I stuffed the phone back in my pocket. "Nope. No worries. I don't give a shit about football."

"I said you can't play because it could kill you. That's me protecting you, Isaiah. I know it hurts, but you're smart enough to see I'm not punishing you, right? You're smart enough to know I'm keeping you out of harm's way, not just being an ass-hole."

"You should take my driver's license," I said.

"Why would I do that?"

She thinks I'm so dumb. She thinks I'm incapable. You don't need to be a reference librarian or a lawyer to find out simple facts. I could do it with my phone while sitting on the back stoop in the cold. "Depending on the source, between six and nine teenagers are killed every damn day in car accidents," I said.

"That's . . . there are teens in cars constantly, all the time. You're not suggesting it's more dangerous for you to drive a car than it is to play a sport where you *will* crash into someone, that *has* caused you to lose consciousness and hear screaming in your ears?"

"You know how many deaths from cars that is every year? Anywhere from like twenty-three hundred to thirty-two hundred. Teens, Mom. Little sons, daughters, sister, brothers, all ripped up, bloody and gone."

Mom breathed deeply. She nodded. "Just stop, Isaiah. I wanted to talk to you about my behavior, not about . . ."

"Hannah is part of a giant parade. She's not special."

"Stop!" Mom shouted.

I stood, quiet, except for my heart that pounded so hard I could hear it.

"I've had a conversation with your dad," she said softly. "I don't think I've handled things very well lately. I forget you're growing up, Isaiah. I think of you as my little boy."

"I'm not your little boy," I said.

"I know. You'll be eighteen on Tuesday. You're two years older than Hannah will ever be."

"I'm not your anything. I'm not yours," I spat. "I am mine, do you understand?"

Mom's red face turned pale. "Yes. I get it, Isaiah. I've been overstepping boundaries lately, but only because I want you to be safe. This thing with football. You have every right to be involved in that decision. I can't tell an eighteen-year-old what to do. . . ."

"Too late. You can't tell me anything," I said. "I'm not a piece of shit."

"I was just angry. Surprised. I said that because I was surprised."

"You said that because you're a piece of shit, Mom."

I walked out of the house. It was the wrong way to go. I should've gone into the garage to get my bike. The garage door was down. I walked around back. The back door was locked. I considered kicking it down. Felt the strength in my body to kick it down. I reared back and kicked with all my force. The doorframe exploded in, ripping wood and taking the whole lock mechanism off with it. The door bounced in on its hinges, crashed, then slammed shut. I shoved it open and went in and grabbed my bike.

As I pulled it out, Mom flung open the interior door. "Isaiah!" she shouted. "What in the hell are you doing?"

"Shut up," I said.

I pedaled away.

For years, there had been two of me. Isaiah who learned to hold it together and practiced the monoculture of football, stayed quiet after all the assaults and insults: the deaths, the divorce, the manipulation and control, and the other Isaiah who was tuned in, filled with rage, and ready to act on it if the cage he'd agreed to climb into ever broke.

That Isaiah wanted nothing more than to fight.

Good Isaiah was still trying, though. Good Isaiah hoped to find Joey Derossi.

CHAPTER 28

OCTOBER 6: TO GRACE

I rode my bike around the block. I was scared. I'd broken the door to my house. What else would bad Isaiah, lizard-brain Isaiah, "do it" Isaiah break? I needed to be far enough away that I couldn't hear Mom if she shouted for me. I didn't want to hear her.

I called Joey. His tape answering machine in his little trailer picked up my call. I left a shaky-voiced message. "Hey, bro. Looking to work. Could use some activity. Please call me back." I waited for a moment but didn't hang up. "Really, really. I could use a cold dose of Derossi, okay?" I said. Then I hung up.

I rode away. Something made me turn back. I saw Mom race around the corner in her Subaru, going in the opposite direction from me. Where would she be going so fast?

Where would I be going? Try to find Joey's Saturday work site? If I rode all the streets of Bluffton, would I spot his truck? Unfortunately, he did about half his gutter and painting work in little towns around southwest Wisconsin. He could be anywhere. Where would I go if I followed my lizard brain?

Grace smoked a cigarette in Grandma's backyard after 3 a.m.

Why wouldn't I go to Grace? Because Dad told me not to?

I rode my bike around the corner to the next block, then climbed a small hill (my heart pumped harder than it should because I hadn't been working out enough). There were no cars at Grandma's house. Not Grace's. Not Grandma's. On a Saturday? Grace was at Dairy Queen according to the calendar on Grandma's wall.

It only took me ten minutes to make it across Bluffton to the Dairy Queen. Small towns are strange. Places feel far apart in your head. Dairy Queen is really on the other side of town. They are not far apart in truth. I'd biked probably two miles in ten minutes.

Grandma's car was not at Dairy Queen. Grace's was.

I pulled my bike up to the drive-through ordering menu.

"Welcome to Dairy Queen. How can I help you?" a squeaky, pubescent male voice asked.

I paused for a moment, then said, "Could you get your manager, please? I found mouse shit in my blizzard."

There was silence for a beat. "Um, okay? Are you sure they aren't chocolate sprinkles? Those get in stuff sometimes

155

because we have a lot of chocolate sprinkles in here right by the window."

"I know goddamn mouse shit when I see it," I shouted. "Have the manager meet me out front."

I rode away from the drive-through. A car pulled in behind me.

I parked at the corner of the store and peered around to the front door. It took a minute or so, but Grace came out. She looked around, took a few steps forward, and shaded her eyes, surveying the parking lot. She held that position for maybe five seconds, then turned to go back inside. I had to say something. My heart pounded.

"Hey!" I said, using all my breath.

Grace turned and looked at me.

"Oh," she said. "It's you."

"It's me. Come here?"

She didn't move right away, but then took one step, then another. She got to me, slid around the corner so no one could see her from the windows in the front. "What are you doing?" she asked.

"Visiting," I said.

"You said that about the mouse poop in the drive-through?" she asked.

I nodded.

"We don't have mice in the store," she said. "Not anymore."

"Good. Did you see me?" I asked.

"Depends on what you mean," she said.

"Not when I was behind the store, but when I was in the kitchen and you were there?"

She nodded. "Two times," she said. "Once in the day, once in the middle of the night last night."

"I saw you, too," I said.

She nodded. "So?" she asked. "So what?"

"So?" I said.

"So you're a little messed up or something," she said. "That's what Gin thinks. Got injured. Got your footballs in a bundle. Something like that."

"Not really that, but yeah. Maybe. I'd like to talk to you about this. About what's been going on."

"Going on with who? With you?"

"With both of us, I guess. You know, you with my grandma and my dad and with the ACT and everything."

Grace turned a dark shade of red. "I don't know why you would know about my ACT score."

"I don't know why you spent the night at my grandma's house."

Grace took a breath. "At two p.m. I've got three on staff. I could leave the store for a while. But I have to come back to close later."

"Where's Grandma?"

"Up in Madison. She and Delores have tickets to the Badgers game."

"I'll be here at two. See you then," I said.

Grace nodded. She went back into the store.

I had to kill an hour and twenty minutes. My phone had been blowing up. Mom, Dad, and random texts from Riley and Twiggs about what the hell I meant when I said I wasn't playing anymore. No calls from Joey.

I pulled my bike up the hill behind the store and hid it underneath the bush where I sat earlier in the week. I lowered myself down next to it. My phone buzzed again. Text indication. Not Joey. I shut my phone off and lay down. White clouds crossed the blue sky. It was chilly. I pulled the hood of my Bluffton football sweatshirt over my head and shut my eyes.

When I opened my eyes, Grace was standing over me.

"Is it two already?" I asked.

"No. Your parents are looking for you. They just called."

"Did you tell them I was here?" I asked.

"No," Grace said. "What's going on?"

"I broke the garage door. It's no big deal. Can we please get out of here for a little bit?"

"Yeah. Okay. It's cold. Nels and Molly can hold up until Caitlin gets in."

"Nels?" I asked.

"Yeah. That's his name. Get over it, Isaiah."

Five minutes later we were in Grace's car. It wasn't the same car she drove before. It was just as crappy, though. This one was an old Chevy Aveo that sputtered when Grace pressed the accelerator. The interior of the car felt like home, though. It smelled like Grace (cigarettes, shampoo, and ChapStick). That's where I wanted to be.

She got onto 151 heading east. "I don't know where I'm supposed to go," she said.

"Go anywhere. Go to Belmont Tower."

She shook her head slightly. "I'm not into some kind of booty call, okay? We haven't talked for two years, so whatever you're dealing with must be rough." She swallowed hard. "And I care about you. What can I do for you that won't cost me my dignity, Isaiah?"

It just popped out. "Dad said that you said that I saved you from committing suicide. What does that mean? How did I do good back then?"

"Huh," Grace said. "Remind me not to tell your dad anything."

"I should know about that shit, okay? I should've known before now. We talked for hours and hours back then. And now I need to know. I should be told if I've had any value at all in the world."

"You don't know you have value? Are you kidding?" Grace asked. "Why is that?"

"Because," I said.

"You're you. Everybody knows you. You're the football player and the teen of the month on the shopper over at the grocery store. Why would you ever think you have no value?"

"Because I thought I was a piece of shit back then, when we were together, but find out maybe I'm a piece of shit now and maybe I was just fine then."

"No," Grace said. "You were definitely a piece of shit back

then, except you were nice and you liked me even when I was an asshole, which I really, really needed."

"I didn't like you. I loved you. Let's go to Belmont Tower."

"No, Isaiah." Grace turned the car to the left, onto one of the last streets before Bluffton becomes the open country. "I'm not interested in doing you. Not remotely."

"I don't want sex. That's just where we used to go. I want to be me and you from before all this."

"From before you got your shit together? From back when you cried all the time?"

"My shit together is fraudulent. Completely. I pretend to have my shit together so my mom doesn't die of sadness."

"So you don't really like playing football and doing well in school and not being drunk and broken all the time," Grace said. She was blushing. Tears were rising in her eyes.

"No. I don't know if that's true."

"What is true?" Grace asked. "Because you're kind of my hero for not being what you were. If it's all bullshit, I would really like to know."

"I'm having doubts and . . . I guess I want to be with my old self and with you."

"I don't want to be that Grace," she said quietly. "I hate that Grace."

"Okay." I thought about the ghost town with the crooked gravestones. "Can we go to Hannah, then?" I said.

"She's dead."

"Out to where the accident happened. I haven't ever gone."

Grace didn't say anything for a second. Then she nodded.

"Do you know where it is?"

"Yeah," she said. "Sort of."

It took us about fifteen minutes to get there. Even though I'd never been to the spot, I'd studied it on maps so many times I knew the route by heart. I could picture the curves in the road in my mind. I could picture the changes in elevation, the rise that would have made it impossible for the drunk guy, Steven Hartley, to see another car roaring down the perpendicular road, to hear fairy bells coming from the car. The only words Grace and I exchanged on the way there were directions.

Grace pulled over onto the shoulder near the intersection. "This is it, huh?" We both stared at the dilapidated roadside shrine in front of us.

"Yeah," I said after a moment. "This is it."

We got out. Walked ten steps along the road.

Someone had put up a cross there on the southwest corner where County Road G crossed Country Road E. That's about where what was left of Ray Gatos's car must've ended up after the collision. For a while, it seemed, kids came out and left things. But not recently. A couple of moth-eaten teddy bears remained, easily visible.

I saw something shiny in the tall, dry grass off the shoulder. I bent down and picked up a blue polished stone, the kind Hannah collected when she was a little kid. "Oh shit," I said. "Someone brought her rocks."

Grace bent down and pulled a small trophy caked in mud

that Ray had won at a speech contest. I dug around in the grass more and found several dirty, damaged framed photographs of Hannah and other kids: Tessa Kaplin, Mara Hottenstein, Katie Digman. There were some empty frames with broken glass, too. I found an empty whiskey bottle. I picked it up.

"What the hell? Would someone really leave this at the scene of a fatal drunk driving accident?"

"A drunk would. That's why it's good you're not a drunk."

"I was never a drunk."

"You were on your way. And I was. Am. Flat out. Self-medicating and addicted. My first thought at seeing an empty bottle is, 'Too bad 'cause I'd like to drink some of that.' I'm so messed up."

"I'm injured," I said. "I'm messed up."

I threw the bottle out into a cornfield. It was cold. Wind rustled the tall grasses in the ditch below. I breathed, shut my eyes, pictured Ray and Hannah driving, the Sufjan Stevens fairy bell song jingling. The summer day. The sun going down. Steven Hartley rises over the incline. He jets down the road in the giant pickup truck. He doesn't slow. Here comes Hannah. Here comes Ray. They cross into the intersection just in time for Steven Hartley to . . .

I opened my eyes but was blind from tears. "Oh shit, Hannah. Jesus, Grace. I can't lose you, too. My mom took you away from me."

Grace stepped to me, put her arms around me. "We were like naughty little kids, man. We needed to be separated."

"No, you said I helped you. You told Dad."

"I did."

"You helped me want to live, too. That's good. Mom just didn't know."

"Isaiah," Grace said. "I wanted to drag you back down to me when we started hooking up again. Your mom was totally right to step in. You're lucky to have her."

"But I need you now. So I'm unlucky," I said.

Grace leaned into me. She whispered, "Okay. I don't know what you're going through, but I'm going to be steady. I'm steady, okay? Maybe I can help you get steady."

"You can," I whispered back.

I stood there clutching Grace. We couldn't just stand there forever, though.

A few minutes later we got back in her car. We left the spot where Hannah left her life. I wish we would've gone home. Maybe nothing bad would've happened. Really, if I think about it, something bad was still coming. Time bombs ticked. And I asked Grace to drive me to the Boulder Junction Tap. I wanted to drive the route Steven Hartley took to get to Hannah and Ray.

"After that, I have to get back to work," Grace said.

It was about a five-minute drive to Stitzer from the site of the accident. Along the way, Grace told me that her stepfather had come back to Deb again for the thousandth time (Deb is what she calls her mom). Grace said she couldn't be in the house when he was there. Deb maybe didn't know what Richie had done to her, but both Grace and Richie knew, and it was bad. She feared Richie getting drunk. She feared sleeping in a house where Richie was drunk. He'd broken the lock on her door when she was sixteen.

"You never told me."

"I couldn't tell you. Thinking about it made me throw up."

"So, he did stuff to you?"

"Twice. Once the December before you and me hooked up. Once in May when I was trying to be a good kid and date Caleb."

"I remember May. You were so mean to me."

"Maybe now you know why," she said.

"Does Deb know anything?"

"You try to tell Deb anything bad about Richie. Go ahead."

"Maybe we should beat the shit out of him," I said.

"No. I don't want anything to do with him," Grace said. "Nothing. I might move in with Gin. If it's okay with you?"

"It's great with me," I said. "It's really good."

For a golden moment I imagined both me and Grace going to college in Bluffton, both of us living on the same block, both of us preparing for a life together. My next life.

We pulled into the parking lot of the Boulder Junction Tap, which is one of three businesses in Stitzer open on a Saturday (there's another bar and a Cenex Cooperative Gas station there, too). The parking lot was packed.

"Badger game is on," Grace said.

Any normal Saturday I would've been with Riley and Twiggs

watching it, too. Maybe even up in Madison with Mom and Grandma Gin, attending the game. For four years, that's what I did. Played football, watched it, absorbed it. But outside the Boulder Junction Tap, I couldn't even remember who the Badgers were playing.

"This is where Steven Hartley got loaded and turned himself into a missile," I said.

"Gross little bar," Grace said.

Four dudes stood outside the front door. They wore Badger gear and baseball caps. They smoked cigarettes. One, a large man with a big gut, swayed and had to keep catching himself on the post of the foyer.

"Trashed," Grace said.

"How do they all get home?" I asked.

"Look at all these cars, man," Grace said.

It was probably the wrong thing for her to say, but she couldn't have known it. "They're all going to drive out of here?"

Grace looked at me. She shrugged.

"These dicks don't care about anything."

"I've driven buzzed," Grace said.

"Don't. Okay?"

"Don't what? You've been with me. We drank out at Belmont Mound. How do you think we got home back then?"

"We were stupid kids. And we were messed up. These assholes . . ." I pointed at the dudes smoking. "They're in their twenties. Might be older."

"They could be messed up, too."

"Doesn't give them the right to take someone else's life," I spat.

"You want me to call the cops on everybody?" Grace asked.

"I don't know," I said.

Then it happened. The big guy, the one with the gut, flicked his cigarette into the parking lot, then lumbered away from the front door. He weaved a little as he walked. So trashed.

I leaned forward. "Where is he going?" I asked.

"I need to get back to work," Grace said.

I followed the guy with my eyes. He stopped at a dark blue Chevy Blazer. He leaned into it for a second, caught his breath or whatever, then pulled keys out of his shorts pocket. He pressed a button, flashing the brake lights, and unlocked the door. He climbed in and started the engine.

"Shit," I shouted. And I was out the door and running across the parking lot.

"Where you are going so fast?" one of the other dudes said to me.

I got to the Blazer, ripped open the door, and said, "Really?"

"Who the hell are you?" he asked.

"You going home?" I asked.

"To my girlfriend's. She made a lasagna," he said, smiling.

"The hell you are, you drunk."

I grabbed the collar of his Badgers golf shirt and pulled him hard out the driver's seat.

"Jesus Christ!" he shouted.

I shoved him up against the side of the Blazer. He was easily six inches taller than me. I had to reach high to keep my hand twisted in his shirt. "You don't drive wasted. You will kill someone." Held him there. He was cowed. He just stared at me scared and confused.

It was the other guy. I saw him dash up just as Grace screamed, "Isaiah!"

He leaped at me. I simultaneously released the big dude and spun to the side. The guy flew by, landed, skidded on his chest and his elbow on the parking lot. He pushed himself up fast, turned, and came back at me. This is essentially what I've been trained to do. Shed a blocker. Hit a target. I coiled and jacked him with my hands, knocking him flat onto his back. I leaped on him and pressed him hard onto the gravel lot. Then I was out of my comfort zone. In football the play ends. But the dude squirmed under me. He was heavier than me. He started bucking. I didn't know what to do. I didn't want him to get up. I panicked. I barred my left arm across his throat, reached back with my right, and threw a hard punch into the side of his face. He stilled and swore.

Grace was to us. She screamed something. She pulled me off him. The big guy tried to kick at us. Grace screamed something at him, but I couldn't hear. Adrenaline coursed through my body, vibrated in my ears. I thought I might throw up. This is the feeling I had after I obeyed "Do it." Out of control. Having caused destruction. But what had I destroyed? I stopped a guy from driving away trashed. Wasn't that good?

She dragged me back to her car while more people came out

of the bar. They shouted stuff at us. She shoved me in the passenger side door and ran around to her side, turned on the car, and took off. A beer bottle crashed on the hood.

"Shit!" she cried.

"Oh shit," I whispered. "I might puke."

"What are you thinking?"

"I don't know," I said. Blood bubbled from my elbow. "Got a cut." I raised my arm to show her. But she didn't look.

I pulled my hoodie over my head and removed my T-shirt. Blood dripped onto Grace's seat. I wrapped the T-shirt hard around my arm and tied it tight, using my left hand and my teeth to put my sweatshirt back on.

Grace shook her head as she drove. Tears rolled down her face. "Do you know guys like that? They have guns in their cars. Somebody could've shot you," she shouted. "Not to mention the fact that you could've killed someone yourself. What difference does it make if you kill someone while drunk driving or you kill someone by thinking you're stopping them from drunk driving?"

"I didn't kill anyone." I dropped my head. Rested my chin on my chest. "I wish I was dead," I said.

Grace didn't hear me. "I don't know. I don't know," she said. "This is going to get back to town. Look what I did. Left my shift. I drove with you. I drove you to a bar. I let you get out and do this. Look what I did."

"You didn't do anything. Don't worry, Grace. I . . . I can tell them what happened. I freaked. I shouldn't have asked you to take me there."

"Just be quiet," Grace said.

I got quiet.

Suddenly a cop car, lit up, roaring, burst onto the road in front of us. It fishtailed, straightened, shot past us back in the direction from where we came. I turned and watched it scream down the county road toward Stitzer.

"Who do you think that's for?" Grace said.

"They would've stopped us here. They'd have a description of your car."

"Oh God. Oh God," Grace cried. "I know what happens when we're together, but I went off with you anyway. I deserve what I get."

"You don't deserve anything."

"Shut up, Isaiah!" she screamed.

I didn't say another word. When we got back into town she asked where I wanted to be dropped off. I told her my bike was at Dairy Queen. When we got there, she parked, got out, and walked into the store.

I vomited and cried by my bike.

CHAPTER 29

OCTOBER 6: THE FLUGEL ROCK

I lay on the ground behind Dairy Queen. I didn't know what to do. It was possible the police would be looking for me. Should I just bike to the police station? My legs began to twitch. And then what? Back to eighth-grade Isaiah? Had I already gone back? I couldn't go back. Where else could I go?

I turned my phone on and found a blizzard of messages. Parents, Grandma Gin (who does not text, but texted from the Badgers game), Twiggs, Riley, Coach Dieter, Coach Reynolds.

They all knew the real me now.

There was a voice mail from Joey, too. I could catch my breath there.

I called him.

"You all right, bro?" he asked. "Looks like your dad left

a message on my machine. That's some weird shit, don't you think?"

"Can you come and get me? I need to hang for a bit," I said.

"Yeah, man. I finished this job over in Cuba City today. Lady paid me three hundo! You want to get some pizza?"

"No. I'd like to come to your trailer. I want to hang out there."

Joey breathed in for a second. "Dude. Okay? So. Where you at?" he asked.

"Dairy Queen, but I'll meet you out where County D passes that cemetery. I don't think I should stand out here in the open."

"You're kind of freaking me out," Joey said.

Fifteen minutes later, he picked me up at the St. Mary's Cemetery. Not Hannah's. I threw my bike in the back of his pickup. He asked me no questions. Before we drove to his place, he insisted on stopping for frozen pizzas at Kwik Trip. I slid way down in the cab so no one could see me while I waited in the parking lot.

When we got to his trailer, which is off West View Road, far enough that you can't see the trailer if you're just driving past, Joey turned on the oven.

"Once the oven is heated up, we're twenty minutes from pizza. This is the only time I waste energy, bro, when I'm not sure when I'm going to eat my pizza but am hungry enough to know I can't wait for the oven to preheat when the time comes."

"Oh," I said, but wasn't paying attention to his chatter. I thought about Grace. Were the cops coming for her? Someone probably did write down her license plate number.

"You gotta check this out. I'm building something because of some stuff you've been thinking about."

"Maybe I could just lie down for a second," I said.

"No way, dude. We have to go up to the barn before the sun goes down."

I hesitated, then followed him out to the trail that led to his great-grandpa's barn. Even though it couldn't have been later than four thirty or five, the sun had disappeared behind one of Bluffton's namesake bluffs. The indirect light colored the valley a deep orange. The barn on the property is cool. It's old as can be—maybe over a hundred? The stone foundation—which Joey and I patched over the summer using concrete, cast-off cinder block, and some limestone we took from the shed at Church of the Hills, his great-grandpa's church, which went defunct last May—rises about ten feet out of the earth, making for a cool, open space inside. The wood structure's loft was built another ten feet up, so the ceiling of the first floor is like twenty feet off the ground. Joey opened the door and we entered.

The barn's bottom floor is divided into two rooms. Historically, this first room has been a mess, filled with junk Joey's collected through the years to make art. But now the room was organized, swept. Joey had dragged metal shelving units in. The walls were lined with his junk, but it was all organized into categories: tools, hardware, toys, stacks of canvasses—old artwork people had given him, musical instruments, games and puzzles, coffee cans full of pennies, stereo equipment dating back decades, and more. All the junk that made the barn look like the municipal dump before now looked like a collection in a museum.

"Wow," I said, forgetting my troubles, poking through the metal toys (old tractors and cars) on one shelf. "This is a big change."

"This is just the beginning, bro. This is like my memory, okay?"

"Okay."

"It's like your green notebook, filled with all that shit about who you were and are right now. It's all useful, right? You make an accounting of what you've experienced so that you understand what you're set up to do next. But my shit wasn't organized. It was jumbled like my brain."

"I haven't thought about my notebook like that. Like memory."

"Then you ain't thinking straight, bro!"

"I'll think about it."

"Yeah, dude, do that. Because check this out. I was wrong about your monoculture, about football, okay? Football for you is an effort in the right direction, right? Going someplace even if you're not sure where. It uses all these things you've got inside you. Like your grandpa and grandma freezing their asses off to be at that Ice Bowl football game and how they fell in love because of it and how Hannah got killed and you have all this rage that makes you want to break shit and how your family fell into hell, disintegrated after your grandpa died and your sister died and nothing held the center anymore and football is team, right? It's orchestrated social action and it's scary, because it hurts when you lose, not just emotionally but physically, but you're stronger with your team, your family. Man, I've been wrong to bum on you about those fools Riley and Twiggs."

"Riggles and Twine?" I said.

"No. I'm not going to demean them anymore. They're your brothers. They're the family you had to make because your biological family broke to shit."

"Oh man," I said. "I don't know if I want to hear this right now."

"Buck up, dude. Football is how you took all the energies of your life, good and bad, and organized it and made sense of it and made something beautiful out of it."

"Oh man, Joey," I said. I could feel my jaw tremble. I could feel myself start to cry.

"Don't get all bent, bro. I'm using you as an example, okay? I can't live in the past like I have been. Yeah, this is my great-grandpa's barn and he was a serious badass who raised my grandpa who was a sweet dude who raised my dad, who got sick and died way too young and, yeah, my family, which is pretty much just me at this point, only owns a few acres out of the three hundred and twenty we once did, but look at what I have?" He gestured with his hand. "Half this shit is from my family, half this shit I collected because it reminds me of my family."

"It's so cool."

"It's not anything until you make something of your inheritance, though, right?"

"Yeah?" I said.

"So that notebook of yours, that football talk got me thinking one way. And then my damn cocktail drum set got me thinking another way."

"What about your drum set?"

"Shit, my drums. You know my grandpa played the flugelhorn in a damn oompah band?"

"I don't know what an oompah band is."

"Polka, bro. He and the Krauts around here played the oompah music and all the farm ladies danced till the sun went down."

"That sounds good. I like that."

"Me too, man. And my dad? Before the sickness took him, he was like this incredible heavy metal drummer, okay? There are pictures at the high school of him in the pep band, but that wasn't his joy. He and some dudes from Hazel Green had a hair metal band and they played every weekend. The Bluffton girls and the Cuba City boys, they all put on their makeup and hairsprayed their hair up to the damn moon and tied bandannas on their ripped jeans and headed out to head bang till the sun went down. Actually, probably more until the sun came up for that crew."

"Cool."

"Hell yeah, it was. And this is my legacy, you know? That music, which I can't play—that's what the drum set has taught me, I have no damn rhythm."

"Ha," I laughed. Joey makes me laugh even when I'm broken.

"And this land and all these incredible pieces of junk that I've just let lie on the ground, like with no respect. I have to respect my inheritance!"

"Yeah?" I said.

"So, check this out." Joey opened the door between the front room and the back room. "This is my football, dude. And I was wrong. It's not monoculture. It's all my culture coming together to build one great thing."

I was expecting to see greatness, but what I saw was a low wall built of stones running across the room toward the back. It was only about a foot high.

"You making a stone . . . something?"

"You can't see it?" Joey asked. "Use your imagination."

I tried, but I couldn't see anything but the little wall. "Huh," I said.

"It's a stage. I'm making a stage. This barn has just been sitting out here for years gathering the dust and detritus of my soul. I'm bringing it back to life. Weirdest music venue around, okay? I even pulled some building permits from the city. They're down. I'm going to call it the Flugel Rock, after Grandpa and Dad. And that stage? It's not even close to done." He walked to the back and opened the door. A giant pile of blond stone sat behind the barn, ready to turn it into a beautiful stage. "I paid Jerry Wiegel seven hundred fat ones to unload the rock here—I'm going to need your brawny help lifting these mothers. I can't move most by myself, not even with my wagon."

"Of course, I'll help. If I'm not in jail."

"What?"

"Nothing, nothing."

He pointed to the pile. "These rocks, bro, they're the bell tower from Church of the Hills. My great-grandpa built that tower! These rocks held up a four-hundred-pound bronze bell that finally cracked after seventy-five years or whatever. Then what? The rocks had no purpose. And the church died, so they just stood out there like some grave marker? No way. They're going to hold people making beautiful music, just like they held that bell calling everyone to worship the great eyeball in the sky all those years."

I walked over, bent down, and put my hand on one of the cut stones. "The tower is never for nothing. The pieces can be reused for a new purpose."

"Yeah, man!"

"The energy isn't destroyed. It just changes form," I said.

"You can't destroy the energy!" Joey said. "Let's go cook up those pizzas."

"I love your barn," I said.

"Yeah. Me too, bro," Joey said. "Flugel Rock. Get it?"

"I get it," I said.

CHAPTER 30

OCTOBER 6: THE CRIMINAL

After we downed the two frozen pizzas, Joey said it was time for tunes and reflection.

He hadn't asked why the hell it was my dad had left a message on his answering machine. I didn't let out that I'd earlier been in a fight and had punched some Badger-clad jackass who tried to jump me for jumping his pal. Joey had, it seemed, noticed that my knuckles were scraped up and that I'd tied a bloody T-shirt around my arm, but he didn't push me about this odd constellation of details. He waited for me to talk about it.

We sat in the living room of his trailer, an ugly plaid couch and an ugly plaid love seat. I drank root beer like we always did when I visited (Joey kept Potosi Root Beer on tap in a "kegerator"-style refrigerator in the living room). The place was much neater than usual, which I mentioned to him.

"Dude, it's from you. More inspiration from your green notebook. I'm cleaning up my life!" He put a *Getz/Gilberto* jazz album on the record player that sat on a wood console. The music was Brazilian, he told me. From 1964. Over fifty years old and it still sounded good.

"You take such good care of your music," I said. "My dad has old records, but they're all messed up. They skip. I don't even know why he keeps them."

"The covers probably contain memories."

"He doesn't take care of his memories."

"My gramps and my dad did, you know? They were lovers of the actual music on this vinyl. You couldn't even play one of these suckers without cleaning it before and cleaning it after. They cared about shit more deeply than most people do."

I let that comment hang in the air for a moment, then got to it.

"Hey. I don't think you should talk about me as your inspiration, Joey," I said quietly. "I don't think I'm worthy of that. I mean, I know I'm not."

"You mean, that shit you said about going to jail?"

"Yeah. That's part of it."

"Did you do something bad?"

"I fought some drunk guys. I beat them up."

"Oh!" Joey said. "That's not nearly as bad as I figured. Nice! You can work that shit out with the cops, no problem."

"I'm in a bad place, though."

"Dude, I know. Your dad left that message. He was real worried about you because you kicked the shit out of a door and then ran away like a crazy man."

"He said that?" I asked.

"He said something like that, yeah," Joey said.

"It's true."

"Listen, can I tell you something while we're getting real about this?"

"Yeah."

"Before I came to get you at the cemetery, I called up your old man and let him know I was going to pick you up. I told him I'd let you hang out here for a while, but I'd make sure you got home, too."

I sat up straight. "You did what?" This didn't feel like Joey. This didn't seem right. This broke the rules for us. "Why, man? Why would you do that?"

"He was worried, dude."

"Everybody's worried. Mom's worried all the damn time. But this is my life, not his. It's not hers. It's mine," I said.

"Yeah," Joey said. "But I hate to hear a dad be worried. My dad didn't get to worry about me and I think he'd want to know I'm okay. Plus, this . . ."

Anger began to boil in my gut.

He went on. ". . . I think my brain recently myelinated, you know what I mean? I feel like my frontal lobe turned adult in the last couple of weeks. That's one weird-ass feeling, I tell you that. Having your brain suddenly grow?"

I stood up, drained the root beer in my mug. "I have to go."

Joey placed the record cover he was holding down on the console. He spread out his arms, smiled. "Come on, bro. Just chill. There are some more things I want to tell you."

"No," I said.

"Sit down."

I didn't.

"That green notebook you've been writing in? You know how much that's meant to me? How much that's made me think?"

"About how you want to screw me over?" I said, mouth getting dry, skin itching.

"Chill. Come on. You've inspired me with your process, man. And it's good, getting that Isaiah Sadler life in my lungs. That air makes my nut clear as a bell." He pointed at his head. "I'm new, bro. I'm not just going to be weird Joey the hippie dude in the trailer."

"That's too bad. He was the best person I knew."

"Well, I'm still him, but more. Because I'm not going to be *just* anything, okay? I'm going to be Joey Derossi the king of all goddamn hippie trailer dudes in the whole world. That is my path forward with this barn project. I have you to thank for that. You're a quiet leader, Isaiah Sadler. You lead by example. I'm just following your lead, okay?"

Just then, a set of headlights pulled up the drive outside Joey's trailer. We both turned and looked out the window.

"Who's that?" Joey asked.

"Is it my dad?" I asked.

Suddenly the trailer filled with flashing blue and red light.

"Whoa," Joey said. "Wasn't expecting that. Cop cruiser. Your dad must've told the cops where you were!"

"No. No. This can't be happening," I said.

Joey held up his hands in that universal signal to chill the hell out. "It's cool. It's going to be fine, okay?" Joey said.

Someone pounded on the door with a heavy object.

"Don't let them in," I said, shaking. "I don't want to do this again. Please, man."

Joey laughed. "You fought with some drunks, bro. No big deal. Happens every night down at the bars."

The pounding came again.

Maybe I should've welcomed speaking to the cops. I could tell them that I tried to stop a drunk driver but was attacked by another guy and only defended myself from that attack. Yeah, it was a stupid move on my part, but that was the truth. I was trying to save people. And I could tell them Grace just drove me, had nothing to do with it. I could tell them I was sorry. I could apologize to the guy I punched. . . .

But no. Maybe I have some form of PTSD? Instead of facing the cop, I freaked out like when I was a little kid.

I ran to the back of the trailer, Joey Derossi's bedroom.

Joey shouted, "Just stop that shit."

The windows in this bedroom were the size only a cat could wriggle through. I ran to the bathroom. I'd helped Joey install a wall full of glass bricks in there. No way out. I cut back into the living room, where the cop now stood.

"Isaiah," the cop said.

"No," I replied.

"No?" the cop asked. "You're not Isaiah?"

"No. I won't go," I said.

"That's not an option," the cop said.

"You can't arrest me," I said.

"Nobody said anything about arresting anybody," the cop said. "Come on. Let's go."

I still had the heavy root beer mug in my hand. Like a wild idiot on a reality TV cop show, I lifted it above my head. "No!" I shouted. "I won't go."

"Bro," Joey said. "What in the hell are you doing?"

I threw the glass mug at the floor with as much force as I could. I don't know what I was thinking. If I wanted to hit the cop, I'd have thrown it at the cop. If I wanted to shatter it, to create a diversion so I could run out the door, I'd have thrown it at the wall. But I flung it at the floor? At the carpet?

It bounced left off the floor and crashed into the console stereo's right speaker, breaking the delicate woven wood lattice, cracking the wicker speaker grille behind, causing whatever mechanism the grille protected to pop and then let out a loud, continuous hiss.

"Oh shit!" Joey cried. "You killed Grandpa's stereo!"

"I'm not leaving," I yelled at the cop.

"The hell you aren't, dude," Joey shouted. "Get out of here. Go with the cop, man!" Joey knelt next to the speaker. He pushed his fingers into the hole I'd made, pulled out a piece of broken wood. "Look what you did."

I'd never seen Joey sad. Not once. When Joey talked about his dead father or grandfather, he was always happy. He told good stories about their lives. When he talked about his mom, who left town with a truck driver and now waitressed at a Norwegian troll-themed restaurant in Mount Horeb, he got a glint of joy in his eyes. "She wears an elf hat, dude!" When Joey talked about Hannah and Ray Gatos, it was always about a memory that made Joey laugh, not about death, not about sadness.

Now he blinked at me, brokenhearted, tears in his eyes. It took getting involved with a disaster like me to find out the meaning of unhappiness. I couldn't take it. That was enough.

I held out my hands to the cop and said quietly, "Cuff me. Okay? I don't know what the hell I'm doing."

"Come outside and get in the car, you fool." The cop turned, without cuffing me.

"I'm sorry, man," I whispered to Joey.

"Get out, dude," he said.

I followed the cop out, leaving Joey and his cracked stereo behind.

CHAPTER 31

THE FIRST ARREST: PARALLELS

I tried to write about this in my green notebook during the summer, but I couldn't get through it all. I think this was the most scared I ever was.

> There was a mowing shed in Smith Park.
> Reid and Ben had run right after the three boys dumped the gasoline and set fire to the Christmas trees. Isaiah, for some stupid reason, couldn't leave the site. He watched the flame lick upward through branches of these big trees, which had been carted in (there were only hardwoods in Smith Park, so the Christmas display relied on five cut pines in big metal stands). It took a few minutes for the fire to engulf the entirety of the evergreens. The wood crackled

and popped. The yarn ornaments elementary school kids made for the display let off so much smoke as they burned. The city's silver and red plastic bulbs melted and dripped.

The strings of lights somehow stayed illuminated, though.

In the flames, Christmas lights blinked as if nothing at all was happening.

Isaiah couldn't take his eyes off them.

Then he heard shouts. Even though it was after midnight, the fires grew large enough to attract attention. The Christmas-light spell broke. Isaiah turned to see neighbors across the street coming out of their houses.

He sprinted deeper into the park, toward the mowing shed he'd broken into earlier to get the gasoline. He entered the shed, pushed his way between a wall and a large John Deere riding mower. He backed himself into the corner and slid down, folding himself into a tight, tiny spot on the floor between the back of the mower and the wall.

He tried not to move. He tried not to breathe. His position in the tight spot made it difficult to breathe, in fact. The fire nearby burned so bright it illuminated the corners of the door. Isaiah shut his eyes.

He pulled in a gulp of air. Something in the interior of his winter coat crackled. He gulped another breath. Whatever it was crackled again.

He hadn't worn the winter coat since the previous winter. The weather up until Thanksgiving Day, two days *before, had been unseasonably warm, and Isaiah refused to wear anything warmer than his hoodie. But when he was about to leave, to stay overnight at Ben's house, Dad—who didn't want him to go at all—had refused to let him out the door without putting on his warm coat. The temperature had dropped into the twenties during the day.*

He gulped another breath. The thing in his coat crackled again. He unzipped the top of his zipper and pushed his right hand inside. He had an interior pocket. He had to unzip that, which wasn't easy given his balled-up position. He managed to get the zipper open. Inside the pocket, he felt a wrapper of some kind. He pulled it out.

Reese's Pieces.

The previous Easter he and Hannah had sat in church with Grandma and they'd passed Reese's Pieces back and forth while the pastor droned on about rebirth, the resurrection, rising from the dead.

Sirens began to wail in the distance. Their volume increased.

Isaiah opened the package of Reese's Pieces. On Easter morning, the earth in Bluffton, Wisconsin, had been covered with several inches of new snow. He'd worn his winter coat for the last time that spring. This little package of half-eaten Reese's Pieces was the same one he and Hannah had passed back and forth in church.

"Died for your sins," Isaiah said.

He pulled off his gasoline-smelling glove and dropped

three Reese's Pieces into his warm hand. He popped the Reese's Pieces into his mouth, chewed. They were crunchy. Tasted the same as before.

"On the third day he rose again," Isaiah said.

The sirens screamed. He could see other lights competing with the light of the fire. Red lights. Blue lights. The sound of a car accelerating. Shouting.

"He ascended into heaven," Isaiah said.

The lights kept blinking in those burning trees even as the flame consumed them.

Red lights. Blue lights. Headlights. A cruiser pulled up in front of the mower shed.

Car doors opened and slammed.

There were voices. Chatter on a police radio. A pounding on the shed door.

"Hannah," Isaiah said. "Help me."

"We're coming in, kid," said the officer outside.

CHAPTER 32

OCTOBER 6: BACK HOME

The cop didn't take me to the police station. Instead, he drove east along the outskirts of Bluffton, past the swimming pool where I fought kids when I was little; past Smith Park, where I burned the Christmas trees; past the hospital where I went to have my head checked after the concussion; and finally into my neighborhood.

The cop was young, not a guy I'd ever met before through Grandpa. He hadn't said anything the whole ride. When we got near my house, I said, "Why aren't you taking me to the station?"

"For that crap over at Boulder Junction?" he asked.

"Yeah."

"We have your girlfriend over at your house. Mike Meisel from BCA is there."

"Grace is at my house?"

"You and her are lucky. The guy you punched out at Boulder Tap had a warrant on him. He didn't want anyone calling the cops. Left the scene before the sheriff even got there."

"I don't know what's going on, then," I said. "Why am I in a cruiser?"

"Like I said, Mike Meisel is at your house. This is a courtesy pickup."

"But you turned on your flashers when you parked at Joey's."

"Mike said I needed to impress upon you the seriousness of the situation."

The cop pulled up in front of my house. The sun had gone down completely, so all the lights were on inside. There were several cars parked. Grandma's, Dad's, Grace's, and a dark-colored SUV I figured was driven by Mike Meisel, Grandpa's friend from the Wisconsin Bureau of Criminal Apprehension.

"Looks like a party," the cop said.

He had to get out to open the door for me because the back door of the cruiser was locked. When I got out he wished me good luck.

I had no idea what to expect but followed the sidewalk away from the curb. One foot after the other. Where would I run even if I wanted to? Part of me wanted to run. The part of my brain that said, "Do it." But Grace was inside. And I broke Joey's stereo. He was no longer on my team. Riley's dad would drive me right back home if I ran there. Twiggs's parents would probably do the same. And what if I got away, would I run from my family forever? So stupid. Just having the thought to run was so ridiculous.

I entered the house, scared. In the living room sat Mom, Dad, and Grandma. Mike Meisel sat on a dining room chair, which had been pulled in. Grace was standing, pressed against a wall.

Mike Meisel stood up when I came in.

"Looks like we got him, Gin," Mike said. "I'm calling it a day."

Grandma Gin, who was still dressed in her Badgers tracksuit, stood and hugged him. "Thank you for coming by," she said.

"Good luck." He winked at me on his way out the door. All the cops were wishing me good luck. Didn't seem like a good sign.

Other than Grace, the rest of the people in the room stared at me with pale, exhausted faces. It was odd to have Grace there, joining them. Back when we were Bonnie and Clyde, she was on my team, not theirs.

"So?" Mom finally said. "You're not dead." Her lower jaw began to tremble.

"No," I said. "I'm fine."

"You look like shit," Grandma Gin said.

"I'm not perfect. I'm a little messed up."

"Why?" Dad asked. "Will you please sit down and tell us why this is happening? We thought these times were behind us."

"You beat someone up at that terrible bar?" Mom said. "Why would you go there?"

I took a breath and sat on the couch next to where Grace

stood. Grace immediately left, crossed the room, and sat down on the chair where Mike Meisel had been. She wouldn't look at me.

"Time to confess your sins, boy," Grandma Gin said.

"I don't like to talk," I said.

"It's time to talk, Isaiah," Dad said.

"You've all never been that interested in what I have to say," I said. I turned to Grace. "Except for you, Grace. You always listened."

"Please don't drag me any further into this," she said, still not looking at me.

"Leave her alone, Isaiah. She's a child like you are," Grandma said.

That made Grace start to cry. That made me start to cry. That made Mom and Dad start to cry. Not Grandma, though. She continued to glare at me.

"Talk, Isaiah," Dad said, sniffling.

I thought about my green notebook. All in third person, to keep me from frying in my own sadness. Good idea, Joey. Before Joey made me write, I don't think I'd have had the words to say.

I took a breath. "I miss Hannah," I said. "Since summer, I can't stop dreaming about her again. I haven't dreamed about her for years. And she's so real in these dreams. I miss her so much and I'm older than her now, you know? I'm going to graduate from high school. She'll always be in high school. I think that's why she keeps showing up."

"I miss her, too," Mom whispered.

"But Hannah's not all. I miss Grandpa. I miss Christmas and Dad's Hanukkah menorah being out with the Christmas tree, which we never put up anymore, anyway. I miss Aunt Melinda coming down. I miss all of us sitting in a room together and nobody paying attention to me because I'm on the floor messing around with my football cards, and there's food around and everybody is laughing and Grandpa is telling stories about weird cases he's been on and . . ."

"Oh, Isaiah," Mom said.

"I wasn't a criminal when I was a little kid, you know? I was just so jumpy."

"Kids are jumpy," Dad said. "We never thought of you as a criminal."

"I don't know. I liked to dig in the dirt and mess up couch cushions and I spilled shit and made all these messes all the time, Mom, but I wasn't a criminal."

"I know, Isaiah," Mom said. "I know."

"I was just goofy and I just wanted to do my thing and there were all these people around the house talking and laughing and I felt . . . I felt like the world was this really good place."

I swallowed hard. Nobody said a word.

"But then Grandpa was killed. And then Hannah. Grandpa and Hannah. Grandpa and Hannah. This sounds stupid, but I don't know a lot of things that I can trust, okay? I don't know what I can totally count on, right? But I know I can one hundred percent count on death. It's real. It happens. And it can happen any place, at any time. And that scares the shit out of me and it makes me so sad, because I don't even know what it is, except it takes people away. And the absence of those people proves the world is breakable, that it isn't this really good place, that it can all be taken away and it will be, because . . . we all know it will be. What am I supposed to do with that information? Everything is going away and we don't know when."

I looked at Mom and Dad.

"At first, I turned to you guys because I thought you'd show me what to do. Here's what I got: I watched Mom scream at Dad. I watched Dad stop talking except when the pressure from Mom was too much and he went back into his office and broke things."

"That only happened once, Isaiah," Dad said.

"Once was enough, I guess. When I went and did stupid things after Hannah died, did you ever think maybe I was just pulling a kid version of what the adults in my life were doing? I couldn't deal with the pressure of all the death. I destroyed shit. I made death a living thing. You guys have spent years making death a living thing, okay?

"Even you, Grandma. Aunt Melinda won't visit because you're mean to her. And Mom is mean to Dad and Dad is mean to Mom. If adults act so shitty all the time, of course I'm going to think the world is a terrible place. Kids like me and Grace just get taught it again and again, don't we? The world is terrible, filled with nastiness and bad people and then you get the gift of death as a reward! I mean, why shouldn't I burn down

Christmas trees or break windows at a seed store . . . ?"

"What now? What seed store?" Grandma Gin said.

I didn't pause to answer her question. I revved up. Words tumbled out fast.

"Why wouldn't I go to a shithole redneck bar and beat up assholes who are trying to drunk drive? At least my motivation for that is to keep innocent people safe. Hell, there should be a whole football team of dudes like me driving around, stopping assholes from harming the innocent. Where's that team? I want to be on that team.

"The great thing about football is none of that living or death shit matters. The great thing about football is it requires you to prepare for nastiness on the field. It will be violent, okay? It will be so hard. It will totally hurt. You have to use your head and your heart to get through a game with any kind of success. It hurts! But you'll do it with teammates, who might make fun of you sometimes, but who will have your back if they're worth anything. They will fight for you. They will celebrate you when you do great stuff. They will hug you when you mess up and tell you to get back out there and go.

"I can trust death and I can trust my teammates on the football field.

"But I know, I know. It's flawed. It's not the perfect game because what it does to your body is real. That head thing. My bell. I get it rung. I really did it last week. I understand there's a good reason why I shouldn't play. I really do. If I didn't actually believe you, Mom, believe I'd be better off in some ways without it, I might be fine. I'd figure out a way to get around you on this. Hell, I turn eighteen on Tuesday. I mean, I probably can play without your permission if I want to. I definitely can play in college. Keep playing this sport I love, this sport that makes my life make sense. But I know. What if I'm killing myself? What if I'm doing it for a hyped-up kids' game? Maybe I can only trust in death, not my teammates in the long run, because playing football will kill me."

Everyone stared. That made me mad.

"You know who I absolutely can't trust to have my back? You guys. You, Mom and Dad. You, Grandma. What I've learned since our people died is that you all have your own backs. Dad moved into that shitty little apartment, which means I can't stay with him even if I want to. Mom will move me around like a puppet to please her own needs for security, goddamn anything I might want to do with my life. Grandma will shut the door right in your face if you happen to disagree with her on something. Ask Aunt Melinda how that feels."

The three of them stared at me without speaking. Grandma didn't show any emotion, but Dad and Mom looked like they might break. I wanted them to break.

I nodded. Swallowed hard. "Since Grandpa and Hannah, you're all in it for you. You're all crying victims instead of teammates. What am I going to do if I don't have football now? How will I be protected? Who will protect me? You think I'm going to count on you guys for shit?"

"Stop, Isaiah," Mom said. "It's time to stop."

"Don't like what you're hearing?" I spat.

"It's not that," Dad said. "It's all a surprise, though. Have you been holding all this in for a long time?"

"How many years has Hannah been dead?" I shouted.

"Calm down, Isaiah," Grandma said.

"Isaiah?" Grace said quietly, "You do know your dad and grandma have been looking after me for the last year. Really, Gin's been looking after me for lots of years. And she had like half the state police out there looking for you today, too, you know? Isn't that having your back? They're not as bad as all that."

Dad sat up straight and said, "I got that shitty little apartment so I could afford to keep paying half the mortgage on this house, Isaiah. I didn't want you to have more disruption in your life, even if your mom and I couldn't work out our problems. No way did I ever take happiness in being away from you," Dad said. "Any time you want to stay over, you come over. You can sleep on the bed. I'll sleep on the couch, okay?"

Mom held her hand over her mouth. Her eyes were watery, bloodshot. Her cheeks were fired red. "I think you make some good points, though, Isaiah. I really do," she said in a near whisper. "I think maybe we should talk about it some more in the morning. I think I need to rest a little."

CHAPTER 33

OCTOBER 7: BACK TO 3 A.M.

I sat awake on Grandpa John's recliner in Grandma Gin's silent house. When Mom went to bed and Dad left, I couldn't stand it over in our house. After fifteen minutes of pacing in my room, I'd grabbed my green notebook, a pen, and walked across the backyard. I knocked on the front door and asked Grandma if I could stay there.

"As long as you stay away from Grace," she said.

"I will."

"Good. No more messing her up, boy. If she ever leaves in the middle of a shift again, I'll fire her and she won't be welcome to stay here, either."

"She won't screw up without me inspiring her."

Grandma gave me a blanket for the couch in the TV room.

Then she said, "You got your head up your ass, you know it? Can't see what's around you."

"Thanks," I said.

"Good night," she said.

But I still couldn't sleep. The couch, which I've napped on a thousand times, felt like it was made of rock. I turned on the lights, grabbed my notebook, moved to Grandpa's recliner, and intended on writing. But instead I just sat there, looking around.

I felt like such a jerk, such a selfish loser.

The TV room is filled with all that Packers stuff. In a lot of ways, this room is like Joey Derossi's barn, except Joey has lost everybody and has to do the work of organizing the objects and values and memories of that world himself. I still had people. I had a team, really. I had a family, even if it was broken.

Joey thought he had me, didn't he?

A few hours earlier, I'd gone on a tirade about how I couldn't trust anybody. But how could anybody trust me? I let Joey Derossi down. I damaged his treasures without thinking. And why? Because he wanted my dad to know I was safe and wasn't willing to hide me from the police.

What kind of person would Joey be if he didn't respond to Dad's message? What kind of person would he be if he fought off the cops to help me get away?

A bad one. The kind I wouldn't trust. But I could only register my own needs.

What kind of person would ask so much of a friend?

A bad one. The kind who shouldn't be trusted.

For good measure, I broke his grandpa's stereo.

And what was that bullshit I'd spouted about my teammates, about how I could count on them? Maybe it was true, but they couldn't count on me. Yeah, on the field, when I was in top form, I had their backs. But as soon as I was injured (and injury is part of the sport), how did I behave? I lied to them, skipped practices, skipped out on the traditional pregame meal. What kind of teammate behaves like that?

A bad one. The kind who shouldn't be trusted.

I looked down into my lap. This green notebook of mine. I think it did help me figure stuff out. I think it helped me process shit about Hannah and my life and how I got here. But here I am. Senior year of high school. I would be eighteen in two days. Maybe I'd play football again? Maybe not? No matter what, football wasn't a long-term solution. I had a history of concussions. I'd googled. It seemed likely that multiple concussions lead to brain disorders later in life. Did I want that, really? Was this kids' game worth that? Logically, no. Logically, I'd have to stop. Logically, it would have to be soon, even if I disobeyed Mom. I wouldn't be able to practice football forever and what did I have then? The opposite of practice. My actual, terrible life. What did this green notebook filled with reasons why I played football have to give me now?

Bullshit. Nothing. It contained the ghost town, the dead, the crooked gravestones on the barren hill . . .

But I can't live in the opposite of practice, I thought.

I had to move forward. I had to move into the future.

I closed Grandpa's recliner, climbed out, and made my way up the stairs, into the kitchen. There, I dug through a drawer and found a box of matches. Then I went into the garage and found Grandpa's kindling bag (nothing he used had been removed from the garage). I pulled it out the back door of the garage and dragged it across the yard to the fire pit, which hadn't been used in over five years.

I smelled cigarette smoke. I turned. Grace stood there on the deck.

"You're such a busy dude," she said.

"Why are you awake?" I asked.

"Well, for one, your mom screamed at me because I drove you out to Boulder Tap and your grandma threatened to fire me. Oh, and did I mention the cops questioned me about an assault I was allegedly involved with? Hard to sleep after a day like that."

I exhaled hard, looked down at the ground beneath me. "I'm sorry, Grace. I don't know what I'm doing. I mean . . ." I looked up. "I'm going to stop. I'm getting it under control. I won't get you in trouble ever again. I promise."

Grace dragged on her cigarette, then blew smoke into the air. She shook her head and said quietly, "Great. Thanks."

"Seriously. I really, really like you. I won't ever stop liking you and I won't ever put you in danger because of my shit again."

"It's okay, okay? We've sort of grown up together. There are ups and downs, right?"

"Right. I mean . . ." The words hung in my mouth for a

second. I almost didn't say them. But I was so tired of not saying things for so long. They leaped out fast. "You're my family. I love you. I do. I mean right now. I really love you."

A smile spread across Grace's face. "I love you, too, Isaiah," she said.

"Like how? Like a sister?" I asked.

She laughed. "What are you doing out here at three a.m., anyway?"

I showed her my green notebook. "I'm going to start a fire. Burn this thing."

"That sounds like a really dumb idea," she said.

"It's a symbolic act. The past is over."

"That's a fact."

"And I have to let go of it. So, I'm going to burn the bastard."

The screen door behind Grace slid open. Grandma Gin stomped out onto the deck.

"I can hear you two, you know?" she said.

"Sorry," Grace said. "I came out here by myself. I didn't mean to . . ."

"Isaiah, what the hell are you doing with that kindling bag?"

"I'm going to make a fire?" I said in the form of a question.

"The hell you are. You're not burning anything. Grace, put out that damn cigarette. Both of you get in here right now."

A couple of minutes later Grace and I sat on stools at the end of the kitchen counter. Grandma Gin put the teapot on to boil so we could have hot chocolate.

"So, no one can sleep, is that right?" she asked.

"I can't," I said.

"I never can," Grace said.

"I know that. I hear you thrashing around every night you're here."

"Sorry," Grace said.

"I don't sleep much, myself, anymore. But you young people." She shook her head. "You should be sleeping like babies. I didn't carry around the weight of the world when I was your age. I just wanted my own money and a good-looking man. Nothing more."

"You were lucky," I said.

"How's that?" Grandma asked.

"Because your life was simple," Grace said. "It was easy."

"Like when I was your age and my new husband decided the only fair thing to do was to drop out of college, lose his education deferment, and go fight in Vietnam?" Grandma asked. "Can't let the burdens of citizenship fall solely on poor Black kids from Milwaukee, he said, because that ain't right."

"It isn't right," I said.

"I know that. I supported him, even if I thought Vietnam was a piss-poor excuse for going to war. And I'll tell you, it broke my heart for him to go."

"How did you deal?" Grace asked.

"I dropped out of school, too, put my head down, went to work, saved money so he'd have something good to come home to if he didn't get killed."

"And you slept okay?" I asked.

"Like the baby I was," Grandma answered.

She poured hot water over the chocolate powder in mugs. She stirred, then brought the mugs over to us.

"Now our girl Grace, she has a real problem. She's been living in that house too long and there's a bad man that keeps coming back inside. Old Mama Deb can't see the animal he is. Grace can't have a normal day's work if the creeper comes knocking at her door every night. Two solutions to that. Pretty simple. Either you call the cops and get that creeper put away where he belongs. Or, if you can't bring yourself to do that, you get the hell out and you start making your own life. The reason Grace is here right now ain't got nothing to do with you, Isaiah, got it? She's here because I'm letting her stay here until she's on even ground and ready to move forward with her life away from that creeper."

"I know. I understand," I said.

"But you, kid? What's your trouble? That Grandpa John got killed? That Hannah died? What you're dealing with there is called life. Life and death go hand in hand. I could go at any time. So could your mom and dad. So could you. So? What are you going to do about it?"

"That's what I'm trying to figure out."

"What's there to figure? All the good options are right here in front of you and no creeper is coming into your room at night making trouble. What's the damn problem?"

"I don't know. If I'm not a football player, then I'm a loser," I said.

"So be a football player."

"I have concussions. I should probably quit now. Mom wants me to quit and she's probably right."

"If you have to quit, use what you learned from playing, and go get to work on something else."

I sipped my hot chocolate. It burned my tongue. "That's what Joey Derossi was saying tonight."

"Oh ho ho," Grandma Gin laughed. "That kid, huh?"

"He's the best," I said. "He's great."

"He really is a good guy," Grace said.

"Ha. Okay, then. I'll take your word for it," Grandma Gin said.

"I don't know what to do if not football, though."

Grandma shook her head at me, laughed a little. "How about this, Isaiah? You ever hear someone say something like this? 'There should be a team of football players who go out and protect the innocent from those big, awful jerks who do terrible things!' Sound familiar? Maybe you said that tonight?"

"Yeah. Thanks for making fun of me," I said.

"Well, what the hell do you think your grandpa John was? He was a cop, you know? And he was the kind of cop we need more than ever. Tough as nails with a big, fair heart. He treated everybody well—better than I would have—believed even the worst son of a bitch deserved equal treatment under the law. Why, you might say he was part of a team that went out and protected the innocent. You ever think of that?"

"That's what I thought of when you said it tonight," Grace said. "A cop."

"But I'm a juvenile delinquent," I said. "I can't stop doing stupid shit."

"Because you're a kid. Good lord, John was a holy terror when he was in high school. He got into fights, rolled his mother's car, would probably have gotten sent to jail if he didn't get good marks in school. That's part of what made him so good at the job later. He knew he wasn't so different from the people he was arresting. He knew that everyone has that glass ass. He spent most of his time handing out cushions, not locking people in handcuffs."

"I wrote about that here." I pointed to the green notebook. "I wrote about him saying we all need a soft cushion."

Grandma took a sip of her hot chocolate. She squinted her eyes at me. "You got a big, tender heart, Isaiah. You're more like John than anyone else I know. Maybe you should let your grandpa be your mentor? Even though he's gone, there's a lot he can teach you. Maybe you should spend some time thinking of that?"

I sat up straight. It felt like a slap across the face, the good kind that wakes you up. I idolized my grandpa when I was little. I never felt safer or happier than when I was at his side, digging in the garden, or out in the woods looking for birds (he loved birds). He had no problem with me being a dirty little kid. I was more like him than I am like my parents. Why didn't I think to learn from him?

Then another thought crossed my mind. Grandma Gin wasn't innocent. "I will think about Grandpa, okay?" I said.

"Good boy," she said.

"But you have to think about him, too. I want a real Thanksgiving this year. I want Melinda to be there, too. Even if it means Judy Gunderson is with her."

Grandma Gin glared at me. "Oh, I heard your little speech before, Isaiah. First thing I did when I came in the house was to send Melinda a text, ask if we could have a chat this morning."

"Seriously?" I said.

"But for the damn record, I did not get angry at her for goddamn Judy Gunderson, as your mother likes to say. Lord knows I don't want to imagine what my children do between the sheets. That's Melinda's business. None of mine. I got angry at her for marrying that poor fool Tom in the first place. Breaking his heart. Leaving him standing there in that house they bought. Melinda has known what she is since she was your age. How dare she trick that man into marrying a fantasy that never existed? I am so tired of my children and their ugly, broken marriages. I am so tired, Isaiah."

I thought for a second, then said, "Maybe Melinda married Tom to make you and Grandpa John happy, like I do stuff to make Mom happy, sometimes, even though I don't really want to."

Grandma Gin stared at me. "Maybe that's true," she said.

"I don't know what's true," I said.

"The hell with it. I miss Melinda, too."

"You sent her a text?" Grace asked. "You never send texts."

"I've sent two texts today, little girl. I'm a twenty-first-century woman."

CHAPTER 34

OCTOBER 7: 11:20 A.M.

My intention had been to get up in time to drive Grandma Gin to church the next morning. But it was well past 5 a.m. when I stopped thinking, stopped googling stuff on my phone, and finally fell asleep. The curtains in the TV room keep it dark, and no one else had woken me up. Sunday is the only day neither Grandma nor Grace work at Dairy Queen. Apparently Nels is a DQ prodigy and has learned to run the store all by himself.

I went upstairs and had some coffee. Grandma wasn't anywhere to be seen, but she'd made a pot. Grace's car was in the drive. I figured she must still be asleep.

Good, I thought. Grace should sleep as long as possible.

I called Dad, because I'd had some serious thoughts about

208

how I should proceed, had done some research. There was due diligence that needed to be done. There were some things I needed to see to make any move forward. But I didn't want to go by myself.

Dad lived in the shitty little apartment not to escape from me, but so I could continue to live in my house with my mom. That was a perspective that had never entered my mind. I decided if I was going to do what I wanted to do, I'd want Dad with me, because he has protected me (as has Mom), even though I didn't appreciate it. But now I did appreciate it and I just wanted my dad. So I called him. He answered right away.

Turned out, Dad was already at our house. When I got there, he and Mom were sitting at the little circular table in the kitchen. They had a photo album out, Hannah's from when she was five years old. They were looking at a picture of her wearing a Santa suit and crying mightily. They were both either laughing or crying themselves.

Laughing. Mom looked up and smiled. "Hi, honey," she said. "I think we tortured you guys when you were kids. Look at this."

"Yeah. You guys were terrible to us," I said. But I smiled. They were actually pretty great. I was a toddler that year. They dressed me as an elf. I loved that picture. I always loved Hannah, and I'm sure I loved acting like Santa's helper.

"It's lunchtime. You slept in," Dad said. "Very un-Isaiah-like."

"I was up late with Grandma."

"Yeah. She texted us this morning," Mom said.

"Wow. She's a texting machine now," I said.

"How are you feeling?" Dad asked.

"Like I've lived three lifetimes in the last week," I said.

"Sounds about right," Dad said.

"Isaiah, we've been talking. About you and college and your plans for next year," Mom said. "You need to know, I get it. I haven't been open to listening to your ideas, at all. For some reason I got it into my head that it was your plan to stay here and I was just supporting you. It's weird how I've made my hopes into your hopes. It's . . . it's just really wrong."

I looked at her for a moment. The truth was, I wasn't entirely sure what my hopes or ideas were for college at that moment. Part of me did want to stay in town. That wasn't fake. Part of me wanted to leave and never come back here. That didn't seem reasonable. "Thanks," I said. "I might have some ideas about what I want to do, but I don't know what that means about college yet."

"No pressure!" Mom said with a big, goofy, self-understanding smile.

I turned to my dad. "Hey, I've got to go run some errands," I said.

"On Sunday? What errands?" Dad asked.

"Well, maybe just one errand. I want to go up to school to see Kirby. He works on film all day on Sundays. Maybe a couple of errands after, but I don't know. Would you mind coming with me? I'm a little . . . I just want someone else to drive."

"Of course. You got it," Dad said.

"Do you want me to come along, too?" Mom asked.

"No. I want to be with Dad," I said quietly.

Mom swallowed hard. "Are you going to rejoin the football team?" she asked. "I won't stand in your way, but I want you to know I'm still worried."

"I know. I don't know. I have to think more. See something. Due diligence. That's why I want to catch Kirby while he's putting together game film."

Mom nodded. "Okay," she said.

CHAPTER 35

Dad and I got into his car. He turned the key. The car roared to life. He needs a new muffler. He didn't put the car in drive. He stared straight forward for a moment, then turned to me.

"I'm an abject failure as a father," he said. "I didn't set out to be, you know?"

"I believe you," I said.

"When I married your mother, I meant it. I was this young, out-of-place professor in this rinky-dink town in the middle of nowhere and suddenly I find a radiant, smart, hilarious lawyer to share my life with? I couldn't see anything—not a single thing—that would keep us from being happy our whole lives together. I couldn't see what was coming. How could I imagine what happened to Hannah?"

"No way you could," I said. "No way."

"It devastated us, Isaiah. It ruined us. It's ruined me. I'm going to admit something to you I'm not proud of. . . ." He dropped his eyes into his lap. "For a long time, the sight of you and your mother tortured me. I hated seeing you. You were a constant reminder not of your wonderful, amazing, beautiful life, but of all that we'd lost. Your sophomore year, when I finally decided to get out of the house, I applied for jobs back east. I went so far as to go to an interview at an engineering firm in Boston. But the night I came back, you had a game. One of the last ones of that year. I showed up just in time for the first defensive set. And I watched you out there, already calling adjustments, already orchestrating the team. The third play I saw, you shifted the defense after the offense changed formations. When the play started, you shot a gap on a blitz and hit the ball carrier at the same second the ball was handed to him. It was just a regular play, really. Just a good defensive play. But I could tell you had seen it coming just from the way the other team had lined up. I could see not only your athletic prowess, but your incredible intelligence, and I burst into tears, Isaiah. I just lost it. I just couldn't believe I had such a miracle for a son. I called the manager at the engineering company right there in the stands, even though it was almost nine on the East Coast, and I wept into the phone, told him to pull my name from the pool, told him I couldn't leave my goddamn miracle of a son. I can't make it up to you, you know?" Dad was crying now. "We lost her. We did. For such a stupid reason. For being in

213

the wrong place at the exact wrong time. Almost a statistical impossibility she'd be right there, right then. But she was. Hannah was. I lost her. We did."

"We did," I said. "I know. I hate it."

"Listen, listen. It's been a hard road. It's going to be hard. But as long as I'm around and you're around, I won't lose you, too, okay? Don't worry so much. Go be a miracle, okay?"

I nodded. I really couldn't speak. I mumbled something about Kirby and the high school. Dad put the car in drive.

CHAPTER 36

OCTOBER 7: 12:05 P.M.

Kirby Sheldon, the team manager and AV guy, spends Sundays putting together packages of video for us to watch during the team meeting on Monday. I knew he would be up at the high school, in the tech lab, using the fastest computer in there to do his work. He often texted me on Sundays to ask what I thought the defense would want to see from the game before, what we'd want to see of the scouting video he had of our next opponent. It sometimes annoyed me, actually, because I wanted to spend my Sundays eating good food and watching NFL, not answering a bunch of detailed questions from Kirby.

But Kirby was good. And he cared about his job. So, I always answered.

We pulled up in front of the high school, and sure enough,

Kirby's Honda was out front, the only other car in the parking lot. I sent him a quick text and he agreed to meet us at the front doors.

Dad and I followed Kirby back through the darkened hallways toward the lab.

"A little spooky," Dad said.

"I like the quiet," Kirby replied.

The computer was hooked up to a couple of big, twenty-seven-inch screens. Video from the River Valley game sat paused on each. Kirby sat down at the office chair in front of the mouse and keyboard. Dad and I pulled up chairs from other stations.

"So, what are you looking for? Something from Friday? Or something from the scouting video we have for Prairie?" Kirby asked.

"I know this is weird, but is it possible to look at Dodgeville from two years ago—third-quarter defensive sets, specifically—and Oconomowoc from last year? I might want to look at this year's Lancaster game, too," I said.

"No problem," Kirby said. He minimized the window on the left monitor and pulled up a list of years. He clicked first into my sophomore year and pulled up Dodgeville and then into my junior year and pulled up the Oconomowoc game. "Third-quarter Dodgeville?" he asked.

"Yes," I said. "Let's see that one first."

The two games I asked him to find were the two before this year where I hit someone hard enough and was hit so hard that the normal sounds of the world ceased and the sound of a dying girl, or a witch, replaced them. These were not simple collisions that made my sinuses clear, or my ears to ring a little (that ringing happened a few other times, but never made me feel unsteady on my feet). These were hits that knocked myself out of myself for a moment, at least. They were big enough to scare me.

"Okay," Kirby said, "What are you looking for?" He'd brought up the third quarter of the Dodgeville game.

He let the film run play-to-play. It was a rainy night. Lots of mud on the Dodgeville field. I watched a much skinnier Riley rip a throw across his body to a much shorter Twiggs. Touchdown.

"That was sweet," I said. "I think two defensive sets from now. I made three tackles in a row and the third one was hard."

Kirby advanced the video and quickly found the spot. Dodgeville could not move the ball against us. They were totally overmatched. I knew what they were running before the play started, and by the third quarter, I was no longer playing my position correctly, staying in my lane, but just exploding up to where I knew the ball was going to be. Instead of worrying about my technique, I was angling my body for maximum damage on each of the plays we watched. The first two were run plays into the middle of the line. Each of the first two, their linemen stood up our tackles and another lineman got to one of our inside linebackers. Because their quarterback couldn't throw very well, I wasn't worried about any receiver running a route past me. Instead, I became a missile, dropped my shoulders, and used my head to hit the running back with everything I had. Terrible technique. On the third play, I didn't get away with it.

"Slow this one down," I said to Kirby.

"Okay," he said.

We watched a screen pass begin to unfold. I knew it was coming. As the play happened, I slid to my left, crouched, waited for the ball to get delivered into the back's hands, then exploded forward and went at the guy low. One of the reasons I worked so hard to add muscle weight after sophomore year is that my best shot was always to go low against upper-class competition, dudes who were almost always bigger than me. I fired into the back's legs just as the guy drove his left knee forward. My lowered head collided with that knee. The hit flipped him off his feet and onto his side. For a second, I lay on my face on the field, covering the ear holes of my helmet with my hands. The dying girl screamed.

"Did you get hurt?" Dad asked.

"Not surprising," I said. "I dropped my head every play back then. I think I had a concussion on that play, though. That was the first time I heard witch whistles."

Before the play cut out and moved to the next, I saw myself roll over and push off the turf. I stayed in that game. Didn't come out, even though I was unsteady the rest of the way.

"Witch whistles?" Kirby said.

"I stopped dropping my head by the next year, for the most part. But that doesn't account for everything. Play midway through the fourth quarter against Oconomowoc, Kirby."

Oconomowoc runs a spread, gadget offense, with all kinds of shotgun and options and misdirection, and receivers cutting across the middle of the field. It's the kind of offense lots of colleges are using now. I wasn't prepared to track all of it. We didn't see anything like it during my sophomore year. The game against Oconomowoc was in August of my junior year. What happened during the fourth quarter is the only time I've felt any real pain from being hit instead of hurting myself while hitting.

Kirby began to run the video slowly. "Am I close to what you want to see?"

"Yeah. Maybe a minute later. After we fumble and they get the ball and want to score fast."

"They didn't score at all," Kirby said.

"Yeah. I know." I watched Riley drop the ball in the exchange with the center, which gave Oconomowoc possession on our half of the field with about five minutes left. The video cut to the beginning of the next play. Oconomowoc ran all kinds of run/pass options against us. Even when they went empty backfield, they'd often motion a runner into position to take a hand-off right before the snap.

On this play, a running back shot out from the backfield and lined up at receiver. I followed him out there. Then the guy went into motion back toward the quarterback. The play began. I'm sure I was shouting, "Watch reverse," or "Jet sweep," or "Slant left," or something, because they had a couple of running plays and a pass play that branched from this setup. I flowed with the play. The quarterback handed it to the back as he went by. I sprinted to my left. What I didn't see, because I had my eye on the ball carrier, was the receiver from the other side of the field gathering speed, running right at me.

"Watch out!" Dad yelled at the monitor.

Too late. That receiver cracked back, blindsided me, knocked my feet off the ground, knocked my helmet half off my head. I crashed to the turf right as Knutson, our outside linebacker, tackled the running back after a couple-yard gain. I'd lined my defense up exactly right for just such a play but was still caught unaware and was crushed. It was probably the closest thing I've ever felt to a pickup truck flying through an intersection and hitting a small car before the occupants of that car ever knew what hit them.

I thought of this the next day, when I was sick from that hit. I did not tell anyone. It's likely me and the receiver were each running over fifteen miles per hour. The come-down speed, then, was thirty miles per hour or greater. I took the brunt of that speed because I was straight up and down, not looking, and the receiver had coiled and burst into me. I don't think the collision knocked me out—I jumped off the turf right away to show he couldn't hurt me—but my feeling of being Isaiah was knocked out of my body for a short time.

"I wasn't at that game," Dad said. "I'm glad I didn't see it."

"Brutal," Kirby said. "I remember that. You seemed fine, though."

"I really wasn't fine," I said. "Yale runs that offense."

"What?" Kirby asked.

"Can we watch some defensive sets in the Lancaster game?" I asked.

It took Kirby about thirty seconds to pull up defensive sets from the Lancaster game.

I only had seven tackles, quite a bit by normal standards, but I've been averaging eleven all season. Lancaster intentionally ran away from me. That's okay. It limited the field. I still had a huge impact even if I wasn't the one doing the tackling. We were lined up in the right position to defend against them every single time. That was me. I lined them up. When Lancaster gained yards, it was only because they are good and fast, not because we'd slipped up or had been fooled.

They did run some counteraction, meant to catch defensive players off guard. I was never fooled by that action. I kept my head up. I flowed. I took on blockers with both hands, because I kept them in front of me. Nobody during that whole game had a chance to crack back on me and knock me stupid. I was prepared for what was coming. If I played every play like that, there would be no second impact syndrome.

Then we got to the final defensive play.

Kirby paused the video. "Sure you want to see this?" Kirby said. "It's scary."

"Would you believe I didn't actually see it happen?" Dad said. "I was so nervous for that play, I looked down at my shoes."

"Let it roll," I said.

My teammates did just what I asked. They jammed Dakota Clay, funneled him right at me. And what did I do? I lost my head, acted like a beginner, dropped my eyes, and knocked myself out cold. If I ever did that again against a big dude like Clay, there might be second impact syndrome. There might be permanent brain damage.

Kirby didn't cut the video immediately after the play, like he normally does. Instead, you could see me down on the turf, lying completely still while teammates jumped and celebrated. Only Twiggs seemed to notice things weren't right. He started waving to the sideline while staring down at a lifeless-looking me. And then, boom, I was awake, up off the turf and jogging toward the celebrating sideline.

"You looked dead for a minute," Dad said quietly.

"Seriously," Kirby said.

"Dakota Clay is the size of a Division I tight end," I said. "He's the size of a college dude. Shit."

"Shit?" Dad said.

"I think we have to go."

I thanked Kirby and then we left the school.

"What are you thinking, Isaiah?" Dad asked as we exited.

"I'll tell you in a second," I said, because I was still turning it all over.

CHAPTER 37

OCTOBER 7: 1:07 P.M.

By the time we got to the car, I'd made my decision. I wasn't emotional about it because I think I'd spent the week before preparing myself for some kind of reckoning, even though I wasn't fully cognizant of why.

Dad climbed in behind the wheel. I climbed into the passenger seat. Before he had a chance to turn the key, I spoke.

"Since you brought me up here to the school before freshman year, you know, forced me to play football, or else?"

"Yes. I did force you. Your mother was on board, too, though."

"It was a great thing to do for me. I love it. And since then, I haven't thought for a second what life would be like without football. But I'm going to have to now. I've made a decision."

"What's that?" Dad said. "You're quitting? What about Cornell, Isaiah?"

"I can't play college football. Could you see it on that video? When I was small I went low on ball carriers. I'm as big as I'm going to get, probably. Playing at one sixty-five is fine in high school, but I don't want to be on a college field at one seventy or whatever. I don't want to have to go low to take players out, because I will. I'll succeed at the next level, and that means going low against bigger players, dropping my head, probably hearing more witch whistles."

Dad nodded. "I'd be afraid, too."

"No, I'm not afraid. Not really."

"Really?"

"No. Getting hurt doesn't scare me. My sister is dead, you know? What do I have to worry about? If she can die, so can I. Fine. Right? We'll all die. There are pickup trucks and intersections those trucks might blow through all over the world. I could get injured or killed tomorrow for no apparent reason, right?"

Dad laughed, then said, "I can't believe I'm laughing at this."

"It's just true. It's sort of ridiculous but true. And the Yale offense is like Oconomowoc's. If I go to Cornell and play against Yale, play against the kind of athletes they have, I'll probably get blindsided. Crushed on some play, because I won't see it coming. Fine, okay? I don't care, except, for what? What is the point of getting crushed?"

"For victory?" Dad asked.

"Victory for what?" I said.

Dad thought for a second. "I don't know, Isaiah. School pride? Or to pay for your scholarship?"

"Not enough. If I'm going to intentionally put myself in harm's way, put myself in a place where I will get hurt and maybe get myself killed in the long term, I want it to be for something more."

Dad squinted at me. "What are you talking about?"

"First things first, I need to go to Coach Reynolds and ask him to forgive me."

Dad turned the key. "Where does he live?"

CHAPTER 38

OCTOBER 7: 1:11 P.M.

"Oh crap." When we got to Coach Reynolds's house, we had to park among a dozen cars jamming his driveway and the street out front.

"Family reunion or something?" Dad asked. "Still want to talk to him?"

"Yeah," I said, but it was extra weird.

Why? It was Packer Sunday in Wisconsin. Of course. That's why all the people were there. The game, between Green Bay and Detroit, was the second in a row I'd missed watching. The last time I missed two Packer games in a row was probably . . . never.

I didn't want to make a scene, but I also didn't want to carry these feelings with me any longer without getting them out into the world. During this concussion recovery, I'd reverted to the worst version of myself, to an Isaiah that still apparently resided in me, a sad, angry, broken kid who couldn't see the ways in which he was actually lucky. I'd acted as if this game I love, and my friends, my teammates, made no difference. What a privilege it was to be invited in by these guys, what a privilege it was to be given football. How could I spit in the face of this privilege? I felt so embarrassed and couldn't bear the embarrassment any longer.

I walked to the door. Dad followed me. I rang the bell and Tif, Coach's wife, answered.

"Isaiah?" she said. "Are you here for the game?"

"Oh. Wow. Packers," Dad said. He turned to me. "We really are messed up."

"No," I said. "I just wanted to talk to Coach, quick. Is that possible?"

"Well . . . I guess it *is* halftime. Better go. He won't miss a play."

We followed her into the house. Honestly, I probably would've been scared if Dad hadn't been with me. Probably was a little awkward for him, nerd professor going into a house filled with forty-year-old former jocks. I was really glad he was there.

Coach was stunned to see me. He had just placed a tortilla chip in his mouth when I climbed the stairs of the split-level into the living room. He didn't chew the chip. He stood, chip hanging halfway out his mouth. "Isaiah?" he said, crunching the chip. "What's up?"

"Can I have a quick word with you?" I asked.

Dad and I followed him out of a sliding glass door onto a second-level deck. No one was out there, but the grill smoked and the smell of meat slow-cooking permeated the air.

"What's going on? Are you quitting?" he asked, face red.

"Well. No. I'm not going to quit."

"You're not?" Dad asked, surprised. "I thought that was why we came over."

"No. I'm not going to quit on this team," I said. Watching the video made me certain. I can avoid dropping my head or getting blindsided against high school competition. I just have to stay aware, have to remember. I can avoid second impact syndrome.

Coach gathered himself a little. "Well, that's good. That's good news. I'm glad to see you in one piece. Have to admit I was a little confused yesterday when your dad called. . . ." He extended his hand. "Good to see you, Mr. Sadler." They shook. "When your dad called over and asked if you were babysitting Taylor yesterday. I was like, 'When the hell would I ask one of my players to babysit my thirteen-year-old girl?' Then he went on to say that he'd been under the impression you'd done some babysitting, Isaiah, which I found surprising."

"I lied," I said. "Bad."

"Yeah, you did, didn't you?" Coach said.

I took a big breath. "Long and short story, Coach. I let down the team. I let you down. I've acted like an idiot. Mom told me last week that I couldn't play football anymore, because of concussions, and I reacted like a full-on maniac, got totally lost, which isn't that surprising if you knew me in middle school. . . ."

"I didn't know you, but I sure heard stories."

"That's not how I've conducted myself in high school."

"So I'm surprised by all this, bud," Coach said.

"Here's the deal. I'm not a hundred percent sure I'll be able to play anymore. I cracked my bell against Lancaster. It was a bad one. So bad, I've decided I'm done with football after this year. No college ball. I don't want to get rung up like that a bunch of times and find myself suicidal when I'm forty, you know? Because that's what happens to some guys."

"Yeah, I know, I know," Coach said. "Whenever I forget something, I worry that maybe I got rung up one too many times, myself."

"And for what? For a game?"

"That's all this is in the end," Coach said.

"But I want to try to play. I want to try this week. If I'm feeling okay, I want to finish out the season, because Riley, Twiggs . . ." I had to catch my breath. "Riley and Twiggs have been the best friends a dude like me could ever have. I want to be on the field the last second the two of them play high school ball. I want to be there with them. I want to win state with them."

"Well, I like the sound of that," Coach said.

"Here's the deal, though. I have two conditions."

"Come on," Dad said. "I don't think you're in any position to put conditions on your coach."

"Yeah, odd request, bud," Coach said.

"I have to get this out there, so I can play. Hear me out."

"Fine. All ears," Coach said.

"First, if I show any signs of head trauma this week when I come back, pull me. I don't trust myself. I don't think I can believe what I'm thinking if my head gets messed up. I mean, I feel good and I'm pretty sure I can avoid bad contact, but I need someone watching out for me."

"You bet. We'll be watching out. I won't let you get hurt if I can help it."

"Thank you. Second, don't let me start next week. Make an announcement tomorrow, saying I can't start, telling everybody I lied and made a mess of shit. Let me talk. Let me apologize for my behavior. Is that okay? Please? I need the guys to know I can't get away with shit just because I'm good. I want them to know I messed up and I'm sorry."

"Really?" Dad said. He swallowed hard. "That's, uh . . . honorable, I guess is how I'd say it."

Coach nodded. He clenched his jaw. "Yeah. Okay. You got it. I appreciate you. I do."

"I will play my goddamn ass off, Coach," I said. "I promise."

"My gosh. Watch your mouth. We got kids here," Coach said.

"Sorry," I said.

Coach smiled. "You've always been a little intense, bud."

CHAPTER 39

Iggy Eze, the sophomore running back who showed up this year and made us even that much harder to beat, only lived three blocks from Coach Reynolds. I gave Dad the directions and stayed silent during the few breaths it took to get over to Iggy's house. Dad parked in front of the house and turned off the car. I moved to get out, but he grabbed my arm, stopped me.

"Hey. I have zero idea of what we're doing here. Can you please explain it to me before we go inside and meet this family?"

"You know Iggy," I said.

"I've seen him play. I don't know him."

"Have you seen his dad?" I asked.

"He's the only one wearing full military dress in the stands, so yes, Isaiah, I know who he is."

"He's a recruiter, okay?" I said. "He's the army recruiter."

"What?" Dad said, eyebrows crunching together. "What is this? Are you planning to enlist? I have to say, I think that's a little bit hasty, given the emotional content of the last couple of days."

I exhaled hard and looked down at my hands. What Grandma Gin had said to me during the middle of the night, during the ghosting hour, had hit me so hard.

"Maybe you should let your grandpa be your mentor? Even though he's gone, there's a lot he can teach you. Maybe you should spend some time thinking of that?"

Grandpa had been a screwup when he was a kid? I never knew that. He'd been the most honorable human being on the planet, that's all I knew. What if I really could be like him? What if I could use what I'd learned from football as a base for becoming something new and good? What if I could use my fearlessness to help people?

I looked up, turned to Dad. "I'm not going to enlist right now. I just have some questions. You know, Grandpa John was military, right?"

"Of course I know. Are you seriously thinking about this?"

"I just want some information, that's all."

"The military isn't a joke, Isaiah. It's dangerous and they have to do terrible things, sometimes. I don't know that I like this. It's not a simple answer to what you're dealing with here."

"I'm not looking for the answer. I'm looking for the next step, okay?" I said.

"Okay?" Dad said, but it sounded like a question.

We rang the doorbell, and Iggy answered. He looked totally confused.

"Hi," he said. "You brought your dad over. That's cool?"

"Hey. Listen. I know this is weird, but do you think we could speak to your dad for a couple minutes?"

"He's watching the Detroit game."

"Detroit? You mean the Packers?" I asked.

"Not if you're from Michigan, man," Iggy said. "It's the Lions game, then. But they're up quite a bit. Dad might not be too mad at you."

We walked into the foyer. The house looked almost exactly like Coach Reynolds's, except it was decorated with lots of army memorabilia instead of football junk.

Sergeant First Class Reginald Eze took us into an office down the hall from the living room. "If my Lions weren't kicking some Green Bay butt right now, I might not be so happy to see you," he said, smiling. "Call me Reggie. What can I do you for?"

"I won't take you away from the game for long. Just quick questions. Am I too late to get into West Point next year? Like, too late to apply?"

"West Point?" Dad said. "Seriously?"

"Yeah. West Point."

"Yes. Too late to apply, son. You would've needed to meet with a senator last spring."

"A US senator?" Dad asked.

"Right you are. Exactly. A US senator writes potential cadets a letter of recommendation after reviewing their background very seriously."

"How seriously? Like, if I had trouble with the law when I was in eighth grade would that be a problem?" I asked.

"Well, depends. How bad was the offense? What have you done in the meantime? Have you done any volunteer work?"

"No. Nothing. I just play football."

"Volunteer work would help."

"Doesn't matter, though, right? Isaiah's too late to apply?" Dad asked.

"Well, he could take a gap year and put together an app this spring for the following year or enlist and apply for the following year. All roads are not closed."

"Huh," I said. "I could just enlist. Just do the army. Then come back to college after, right? That's what my grandpa did. He finished his degree after Vietnam."

"Sure. You could go that route. But if you're an officer candidate—and I'm guessing you have some good grades and test scores if West Point occurred to you—there are also ROTC programs that would help fund your education while turning you into a soldier and, eventually, an officer."

"What's ROTC?" I asked.

"Reserve Officers' Training Corps. Good schools all over the country have programs. It's tough. You're a cadet and a student. You drill at the crack of dawn, take military classes and regular college classes in the day, study your nights away."

"That sounds great," I said. And I meant it. Constant work? No downtime? That was the tower on which my football career had been built. Reggie had pretty much described my life when I am at my happiest.

"It's not a commitment to be taken lightly," Reggie said. "Four years of college, eight years after. Four of those can be in inactive ready reserve while you pursue graduate education or a career, but you're certainly looking at active duty for many years of your life."

"Sounds terrible," Dad said.

"No," I said. "Not at all."

"Okay?" Dad asked.

I nodded at him.

"What would he get for that commitment?" Dad asked.

"Tuition-free attendance at a fine school. Money for books. A monthly stipend. It can be a very, very good situation for the right kind of student."

I looked at Dad. He looked at me.

"I need structure, you know?" I said. "I love structure."

"I know, Isaiah. But we should let this idea settle a little, discuss it."

"Okay," I said, but I'd sort of made up my mind already. Energy cannot be destroyed. It takes a new form. This was a form that used the rock I'd stacked for so many years and put me on a path that followed Grandpa John.

Too much, too fast? Maybe. Or maybe things come together perfectly every now and then, like when Dad made me get out of the car and go to freshman football practice instead of sending me back to Muscoda.

That night, after I explained what I was thinking to Mom and Grandma, I looked it up on my phone. Cornell has an ROTC program. The University of Wisconsin has one, too. The college in Bluffton does not.

I'd have to leave town if I was going to do ROTC.

Things were going to change for me.

My energy would take new form.

CHAPTER 40

OCTOBER 9: MY EIGHTEENTH BIRTHDAY

On Monday before the film session, I stood up and apologized to my teammates for my crappy behavior the week before. Most of them were a little confused. They thought I was injured. It didn't occur to them that I'd abandoned them. But Twiggs and Riley knew. I knew. Coach Reynolds knew the whole of it. Still, Coach Reynolds said it was my decision to pull myself out of the starting lineup for Friday's game against Prairie. My team-mates have my back. I've been their captain for two years. They wanted me to captain against Prairie, anyway. I think I'm going to do it, captain, but not start. I feel like I need to be punished, but I also don't want to let them down.

Even though it was only films on Monday, afterward I went to the gym with Riley and ran gassers until neither of us could run anymore, until we fell onto the wood floor on the edge of puking. "There's my boy," Riley said. "Welcome home."

My head felt fine.

It did during contact practice tonight, too. I don't feel any ill effects from the hit that cracked my bell. That doesn't mean there isn't damage, though. There might be. It worries me. It's the reason I won't play college football, even though I love this game so much, even though the rigors of this game probably saved me.

The truth is, kids die playing football. Thirteen did last year. Most of those deaths were related to heatstroke in hot parts of the country. But four kids died of what happened to me, a serious, brutal hit to the head. Four lives lost and I think about those parents and those little brothers and sisters who will miss that kid forever and ever and life will never be the same for them.

Here's some more truth. Four million kids participated in some level of football in the US last year. That's a giant city filled with American kids. How many of them got what I got from the game? How many of those kids were lost at some point but were saved by the rigors?

I don't know.

If all continues to go well, I'm going to play on Friday. Why? Because. Remember? I wrote this thing and so I remember and I didn't burn my green notebook and now I can't stop reading this thing I wrote. I go over it again and again. The play happened during that game against Glendale, where Cornell's

Coach Conti came for a quarterback but found a strong safety, instead. . . .

The moon is a great, bright eyeball staring down from blackest space. Below, stadium lights make the colors vibrate. Yellow uprights. Green field. White away jerseys. Cardinal-and-gray home. The marching band warms up, one minute to halftime. The guys on the tenor drum sets pound a rhythm that bursts inside Isaiah's chest. Boom. Tick, tick, tick, tick, tick, tick. Bada boom boom. Tick, tick, tick, tick . . .

This is it. Where he has belonged. Out on that green field with the eyeball looming, with the percussion exploding his chest.

He can't help it. He looks up. He says, "Thank you."

And then Isaiah locks in.

The quarterback shouts numbers. Isaiah checks out the action in the backfield. His opponent is faking a run play. Seriously. Pretending. "Be ready for pass. Be ready!" Isaiah cries.

Simultaneously, the opponent quarterback says, "Hut!"

No. No run. Isaiah nailed his call. The quarterback drops.

"Pass! Pass!" Isaiah shouts.

The slot receiver goes off the line slow, like he's not even in the play. But suddenly, like the kid is hit with a bolt of electricity, he explodes forward. Tries to break out of the jail Isaiah built for him. And the kid does get behind Isaiah.

So Isaiah swivels, sprints after.

The quarterback jacks the ball high into the air. Isaiah sprints. The ball must be reaching apex. Isaiah sprints. Must be falling, spiraling, nose down toward the slot receiver's outstretched hands. Isaiah sprints.

Then he digs in deep.

Leaps.

And he grabs that damn ball a millisecond before the slot receiver can.

Gathers, tucks, rolls on the turf.

Comes to a stop. Breathes. There is silence. His sinuses drain.

The sound of the ocean comes. The sound of the wind ripping through ditches on the razor-backed ridges.

He leaps up, ball over his head . . .

The arms I leaped into when I got to the sideline were Twiggs's and Riley's. How many times had that exact scene played out over four years? So many. Twiggs and Riley also saved me.

So, I keep reading the passage, but I also called Coach Conti on Monday night and told him I'd had a serious concussion, and that, in truth, it wasn't my first, and so had decided I couldn't commit to playing football in college. He was disappointed, but said he understood. He said he hasn't decided if he'll let his own toddler son play when the time comes. "I can't imagine where I'd be without football," he told me. "Probably in jail for robbing cars back in my neighborhood. But I also can't imagine signing Tyler's permission slip."

I think about Hannah. She didn't play a dangerous sport. She was just a teenager doing what kids do, and the pickup truck got her anyway. Shouldn't I do what I love, even if there are risks involved? No, I've made my decision about next year. But still, even with all its problems, we're losing something big if we lose football.

We might be on the way to losing it. Participation in the sport is going down. And I'm losing football, for sure.

But energy cannot be destroyed. . . .

After practice tonight, I asked Twiggs and Riley to accompany me to Joey Derossi's barn. Joey's pickup wasn't parked out there and he wasn't in his trailer, which was good. He wasn't in the barn, either, which was better. We had to work fast, because the sun goes down early in the valley and it's getting darker and darker every day. But with three of us working, we managed to move the whole pile of rock from the Church of the Hills bell tower from outside the barn to inside the barn. Twiggs started stacking them at first, but I knew that wasn't good. They all had to be on the ground so Joey could see their shapes, so he could see which ones fit together like a puzzle to build his Flugel Rock stage. We sorted them out by size and shape. About the time I was lifting the last small one up outside, Joey showed up. I could hear him shouting.

"Riggles? Twine? What the hell are you two doing in my damn barn?"

I entered carrying the rock.

"Riggles?" Riley said.

"Twine. That's pretty funny," Twiggs said.

"This is some heavy shit, man," I said to Joey.

I placed the rock on the ground next to others of its size.

Joey shook his head, like he was trying to believe his eyes. He wasn't smiling like usual.

"Got them moved in, at least," I said. "I can help you pile them up for the stage when you need me to."

Joey nodded. "Lots to work with, bro. I can get plenty done now you got all these rocks in here. Yeah, man. Plenty I can do."

"Good," I said. "I'm happy to help, though. Okay? I'm happy to lift all the shit."

We stared at each other for a few seconds.

Then that Joey Derossi smile spread across his face. "I can't believe I'm going to say this," he said. "But I love me some football players."

"Isaiah loves you, too," Twiggs said. "Maybe I love you? I don't know yet."

"Shut up, Twine," Riley said.

We all went down to Steve's Pizza, not for the traditional pregame dinner two days early, but to celebrate my birthday.

They toasted me with their Mountain Dews, and Joey's root beer.

"Today," I said, "I am a man. A man with a glass ass, just like the rest of you."

"What the hell?" Twiggs asked.

"No, he's right," Joey said. "We all got a glass ass. Every one of us damn fools."

Riggles and Twine were not convinced.

At 8 p.m., I was home. It was time for the traditional Dairy Queen Oreo ice cream birthday cake. What was left of my family, including Grace, sang me "Happy Birthday." Mom cried through the whole half-hour affair. Maybe wept softly is the right word? She didn't sob, anyway.

Right after Dad, Grandma, and Grace left, Mom kissed me on the forehead. "I'm sorry I'm a mess," she said. "I just love you. And I can't believe everything that's happened. I feel so lucky you're here with me right now, Isaiah."

And then later, 10 p.m., which happens to be my bedtime, there was a knock on my window. I pulled back my curtain and looked out. Grace stood there bathed in the light of my room. I pulled open the window

"Can I give you a birthday kiss?" she asked.

"But you love me like a sister," I said.

"Shut up, man," she said.

We met around the back of the house. We sat down on the stoop behind the kitchen. The garage door I'd broken lay in the yard nearby.

"Joey Derossi is going to help me fix that," I said.

"That's good. He's good."

"Yeah," I said.

She reached and grabbed my hand. "You think we're done with the craziness?" she asked. "I'm so tired of craziness."

"I hope so. I don't know. Pickup trucks are out there driving around in the country all the time."

"Pleasant thought."

"I'm going to do my best, though."

"Me, too."

"Did Grandma tell you?" I asked.

"What?"

"I think I'm going to join the military. I mean, do college, too. But go military like Grandpa John did."

Grace nodded quick. "Yeah. Yeah. She did mention that this morning. I can see that for you. I think that's good."

"What are you going to do?" I asked.

Grace tilted her head down, gave a half smile, whispered, "What do you mean?"

"Next year. When I'm gone."

"Dude, I'm going to go to school. And, I'll put my head down, work, save up all kinds of money, and maybe, just maybe, you'll have something good to come home to if you don't get killed."

"Ha!"

"I'm just kidding, man. I'm going to school, though. We'll see what happens. You know I'm going to be running some business, somewhere, at some point."

"Dairy Queen," I said.

"I don't know about that," Grace said.

"Okay."

But what if, right? Sure, I could die or Grace could die or her energy could take a different form and she could blow out of this town just like I'm going to. What's stopping Grace from doing great things all over this world? She's so smart and tough and perfect.

But what if? Who's to say? That pickup truck could blow by a second too late to hit me and I'll be home. Grandma Gin could ask me to come home. Grandma Gin could ask Grace to come home to take over the business. What if?

"Your mind is whirring so fast I can hear it," Grace said.

"It is. It really is."

"Be quiet. Kiss me. We're both adults."

I leaned into Grace. Breathed her. It was a really good kiss.

It lasted so long, I thought I could hear little bells chiming in the wind. Those bells. Again and again.

Listen to me.

Please?

Energy cannot be killed. It cannot be destroyed. It only changes form.

We're going to be okay.

ACKNOWLEDGMENTS

Thank you to Ben Rosenthal and Katherine Tegen for giving me this opportunity. I can't begin to tell you how much I appreciate it. Thanks, always, to my amazing agent, Jim McCarthy, who has guided me through ten books. Thank you to my partner, Steph, for making me laugh until I'm exhausted. Thank you to my kids, who are all grown up. When I started writing YA, you were tiny. Now you're dang big and old and smart. I'm just astounded by you and so proud of you. Thank you to my mom for insisting I read, insisting I go outside to play, and insisting we watch the Green Bay Packers every weekend of the football season during my childhood. One of my steady joys in life now is calling you during halftime to discuss what's going on in the game.